AEOTA

AEOTA

PAUL

DI FILIPPO

First Edition

ISBNS
978-1-78636-416-6
978-1-78636-417-3 (signed)

Design and layout by Alligator Tree Graphics.
Printed in England by T. J. International.

PS Publishing Ltd
Grosvenor House
1 New Road
Hornsea, HU18 1PG
England

editor@pspublishing.co.uk / www.pspublishing.co.uk

For Deborah, my eternal mystery

AEOTA

1 GLASS, BOX, CALENDAR, STARS

THE UNEXPECTED TEXT READ:

find aeota yesterday everywhere.

I thought several thoughts, in this sequence:
Okay, I find things. Can do.
Who or what is "aeota?"
Yesterday is gone.
Or is it?
Everywhere's a big place.
Or is it?
And who knew this Methuselah of a phone of mine could display texts?

I carried a Nokia 7650, thick and clunky as a box of animal crackers and now sixteen years old. I had purchased it new in 2002, partially thanks to the hype associating it with the film *Minority Report*. It seemed highly futuristic right out of the box, maintaining its sci-fi luster for a surprisingly short interval thereafter, as most such products do these days, and had immediately aided me in my work to some acceptable degree that compensated for carrying it burdensomely in pocket and learning to use it. But after being forced to take several unpleasant and/or unwanted calls at awkward moments, I came to resent its electronic tether, and was always on the indecisive point of throwing it away. I certainly from the outset knew that I had no intention of upgrading it, stepping onto the endless uphill treadmill of Next Great Gadget. I used it nowadays as I had always used it: to place and receive voice calls, and those mainly to my ex, Yulia. I also checked in with my message inbox when I was away from the office.

Of course there was no longer any official support for the orphaned device. Only the ingenuity of my pal Marty Quartz kept the thing alive.

I had never received or sent one single text in those fifteen years, so the appearance of this message was instantly startling.

I noted immediately that the originating number was one of those generic fake strings of digits you see in films, all fives. Someone was spoofing me. So much for any possibility of sourcing the text.

As I pondered the small color screen, about as big as two closed paper matchbooks abreast, the message disappeared, replaced by a question:

PRINT TEXT Y/N?

Could this sucker somehow have connected itself wirelessly to my office printer?

I highlighted Y and jabbed the worn ENTER button between the left and right movement controls.

From the top of the phone, out of a heretofore-invisible slot, a slip of paper the size of a Chinese cookie's fortune began to emerge. It juddered out with a last jolt and wafted to the floor. I leaned forward half-out of my desk chair to retrieve it.

On it were four symbols that I thought I might have identified positively as emojis, if I actually knew what emojis were:

find aeota yesterday everywhere.

When I looked at the top of the phone whence the slip had emerged, I could discern no opening. However the slip had emerged, the aperture had resealed. I popped the upper back where the SIM card went. No print mechanism met my inspection.

I folded the tiny slip and tucked it into my pants pocket.

I would have to ask Marty about this new capacity of my phone the next time I saw him. Maybe he had retrofitted the device with this new ability.

I spun my chair around to use the keyboard of my desktop computer, which, while not quite as ancient as my phone, had stopped receiving automatic software updates about the time Isabella Rossellini had last been featured in a starring role.

Searching "aeota" returned relatively few hits, just a score of pages, most of links leading to the type of seemingly machine-generated gibberish that apparently constituted half the internet, robot prose to be read by androids. The major sensible usage for the word was as an acronym for the American Essential Oils Trade Association. They had a Facebook page, but their main site seemed to be occupied by a squatter. Well, if they had needed to be found, I had found them sufficiently. I'd have to send them a bill.

5

Mission accomplished, and time for a drink.

I had acquired a taste for tequila, neat, working with another guy on a case involving an arboreal Latino fowl. I wasn't a snob, though—the cheapest kind would do me just fine. Right now I was working on a liter of Old Sandstone brand, ten bucks a bottle, no tax.

The harsh golden liquid thrummed down my throat like a death-metal mariachi band.

Putting the bottle away, I thought about the latest—and currently singular—client employing the service of V. RUGGLES, INVESTIGATIONS.

Juniper Holtzclaw had hired me to track down her missing husband, Holger Holtzclaw. Like some wannabe Bernie Madoff selling a cold-fusion device or perpetual motion machine, Holger had been running a penny-ante pyramid scheme among his friends, neighbors, and relatives, involving the supposed invention of a new ultra-efficient methane-recapture technology that would be sold to landfill operators around the globe. He called his corporation Eurybia Enterprises. Supposedly they would employ all "green technology," so everyone loved it. In classic fashion, every new investor's money had gone to keep earlier suckers quiet, with Holger skimming off a goodly percentage for himself. His ultimate in-pocket take had been about a quarter million—peanuts, really, as these things went. But not to the horde of angry chumps beating on Juniper Holtzclaw's door 24/7, eager to reclaim their vanished IRAs or, failing that, to learn of Holger's whereabouts and take their recompense out of his hide.

Juniper swore she had known nothing of her husband's chicanery, and I believed her. She had given me a photo of the man—tall, saturnine, neatly attired, handsome in a sleazy way—and a list of his favorite resorts in Vegas, Holger's native Austria, and the Caribbean. I had taken these solid clues and, within a mere week, turned them into precisely nothing.

I had run out of ideas, but figured maybe Juniper could supply some. If not, she was always good to look at anyhow, a petite blonde resembling a young Goldie Hawn. And I had picked up a lonely vibe from our first interview, as if she would not be averse to some solaceful canoodling.

As if thinking lustfully of women had summoned another female in my life, Yulia's name and number appeared on my Nokia's antique screen, triggering my lone ringtone, a ghostly sound effect that combined an Yma Sumac banshee wail with some notes from a Theremin. I think Marty had crafted it just for me. It wasn't the most soothing of sounds, but you never missed a call.

"Vee Ruggles, Investigations. If you are looking for a missing alimony payment, you need to contact your bank. Those capitalist suckers are pure evil, and delight in delaying the processing of money faithfully deposited into your account by the man you once called Tigerpants."

"Vern, quit fooling around. I need to see you about something. Today, if possible."

Going to see Yulia always led me into some kind of absurd situation which, while not necessarily classifiable in hindsight as "awful," always proved alarmingly and unpredictably uncomfortable, at best.

"We can't handle whatever it is by phone?"

She sounded more than moderately stressed. "No. Swing by the house as soon as you can."

"All right. Is it okay if I bring my new girlfriend? I think she can get some time off from her *Vogue* modeling job."

Yulia snorted like a young colt, which, believe it or not, I had always found to be one of her endearing traits. And despite whatever was troubling her, she could still match me beat for beat.

"Yeah, sure, bring her along. She can meet my new super-stud boyfriend, if Nascar extends the Charlotte Motor Speedway course to allow him to make a pit stop by my front door."

Yulia hung up and so did I. I stared at the Nokia for a full minute, but it didn't play any more tricks on me.

Dates with two hot women, both of whom surely would not be able to keep their hands off my burly, tequila-powered body. Who said I had nothing to live for?

2 ONE BOURBON, ONE SCOTCH, ONE SNEER

ON THE DRIVE OUT TO JUNIPER'S LUXURIOUS DIGS, I developed a sudden thirst. Having left my bottle of Old Sandstone back in the safety of its accustomed desk drawer just in case my cleaning lady should need a nip, I was forced to detour to my favorite dive, A. O.'s Tea Room. The place had been around forever, and during Prohibition it had adopted the innocuous moniker it still sported, as a blind against snooping Feds alert for the shameful enjoyment of illicit hooch. Depression-era proprietor Arturo Olvidado had hung around till the 1980s, coming to resemble a Latino Grandpa Smurf. Over the soused years I had watched him lose about five inches in height and gain twice that in circumference. These days his son, A. O. Jr., himself no dewy youth, ran the place. In honor of his father, or out of sheer cheapness, he hadn't changed the decor since about 1962. I found the midcentury modern ambiance helped one attain *Mad Men* levels of liquor consumption.

Close to two in the afternoon, the lot outside the bar featured only three or four cars. I joined the ranks and went inside, passing under the dead busted neon sign that depicted a lady's hand holding a teacup, pinky finger extended.

Irascible Junior himself was tending the bar. Before my butt even contacted the stool, he had a boilermaker sitting on the stained wooden counter for me. I slammed it back gratefully.

"You got today's newspaper handy, Art?"

"Sure, Vern. Here you go. Waste your day."

Our local rag, the *Argonaut & Globe*, reflected a merger of two venerable papers that had been forced to lean on each other like two wounded soldiers just to survive in this mean shameful age of sound bites and clickbait. Even combined, their resources were a fraction of what they had been when I was a kid. But I was hoping that maybe some enterprising young Jimmy Olsen had solved the disappearance of Holger Holtzclaw for me, and I could read about it on the front page.

But no such luck. The headlines contained only the usual mix of the inexplicable, the outrageous, and the drear. What an insane fucking world. More and more I felt like we were all racing in a driverless train right over the edge of the frigging immemorial Grand Canyon.

I turned to the comics to alleviate my gloom. Maybe today would be the day Garfield had another out-of-body bardo experience.

Something caught my eye in a strip I normally did not read: *Dick Tracy*. In the first panel, one of Tracy's subordinates at police HQ said, "Hey, Dick, there's someone here to see you from way back when."

"Who might that be?" asks Tracy.

In the second panel the buddy says, "Otto Atone," a typical Dick Tracy goofball name, and Tracy does a spit-take.

In the third panel a mysterious figure is being ushered into Tracy's presence, but his face is in shadows. In the fourth panel—

But there was no last panel. The paper had gotten sodden and been torn off by rough handling.

The name "Otto Atone" struck me as weird somehow. I couldn't figure out why, and after a minute I gave up trying. I got up to leave, and found my elbow grabbed without my implied or explicit consent.

I gazed down to see a squat, shabby fellow who looked like the fellow from the cover of Tull's *Aqualung*, if that guy had been living under a bridge for six months. It appeared his greasy moss-green coat had bonded to his frame from continuous wear. Instinctively, I pulled back from his touch.

"You Ruggles?" His voice sounded like a kazoo being played through a wet sock full of mud.

"Yeah. What of it?"

"I got something for you." He pulled aside his coat and took out a small white box that was amazingly clean, given its mode of conveyance. I flashed for a second on the box emoji that my phone had displayed. Did this package contain the enigmatic aeota?

I didn't immediately reach to take the box. "Who's it from?"

The guy sneered. "You got enemies?"

"Well, not really. Except maybe my barber, as you can tell by my haircut."

"Funny man." He thrust the box at me. "Here, take it! I got better things to do than wait on you. Anyhow, it's not who it's from—it's what's in it."

I accepted the box, which was about as big as a four-piece Whitman's Sampler. The guy turned to shuffle off.

"Wait a minute. What's your name? How do I reach you if I need to?"

"The name's Baxter. Brevis Baxter. And don't worry. We can reach you if we need to."

Baxter was gone before I could figure out how to reply.

That left me with nothing to do but open the box.

As soon as I removed the lid, which came away with a slight resistance and whoosh of escaping air, a not-unpleasant scent—like a day at the beach when the low tide had exposed many living things—poured out.

Inside was something organic that resembled a tangle of moist seaweed shot through with gleams of opal, gray, and purple. I poked it with my finger, and it suddenly deliquesced into a sloppy slurry sloshing around thickly in the cardboard box.

I put the lid back on and chucked the whole mess into the bin by the front door as I left.

If this was a free trial for a bento box lunch service, I remained unimpressed.

3 AEOTA
AND AEOTA

THE MARITIME SCENT ON MY TAINTED FINGER
remained pungent throughout the drive to the Holtzclaw place,
diminishing only gradually by the time I arrived.

Juniper Holtzclaw had held onto a very nice piece of property,
despite all the ongoing litigation against her absent husband. About
six-thousand square feet of mock-Tudor McMansion on a land-
scaped acre in a part of the city where trees outnumbered rats, good
au pairs ranked barely higher than killer Pilates instructors, and
trash pickup happened discreetly down hidden service alleys. I felt
ashamed just parking my twenty-year-old Toyota beater at her curb.
If I got lucky, nothing would fall off it while I was inside.

Walking up to her front door, I suddenly wondered exactly when
the appurtenances of my life had transitioned from modern to
antiquated. Getting divorced hadn't left me with lots of disposable
income, true, but I could have afforded a new phone, for Christ's
sake. But I seemed to have cultivated to the point of obsession some
bias against the new, some inertia to change, a begrudging attitude
toward the present that was only getting more pronounced. Pretty
soon, I figured, I would be living backwards, like Merlin or Ben-
jamin Button.

I thought of a Robert Mankoff cartoon I had seen in the *New Yorker* a couple of years ago. A patient lies on the psychiatrist's couch, the skeptical shrink eying him suspiciously. The nutty guy says, "But I like living in the past. It's where I grew up."

Juniper answered the door herself, albeit somewhat suspiciously, a fair stance given the random irate strangers stopping by at all hours. She had kept the house, but no servants. That was a big comedown.

Clad in a cream-colored cowlneck sweater over flower-patterned pedal-pushers and a pair of those mock gladiator sandals that laced up her shapely calves, she looked like the missing quarter of a million bucks that Holger had fled with. She recognized me, of course, but did not seem overly enthusiastic at my arrival.

"Mr. Ruggles. No news, I take it. What more can I do for you?"

"Can I come inside, please? If I make one more convert for the Mother Church, they'll give me a second wife."

That bought me a chuckle, and soon I was sitting on a dark leather couch in a sunny, over-decorated parlor half the size of Union Station. Offered a drink, I angled for tequila, but got only white wine, which was the equivalent of hoping for sex and instead getting a lecture on social justice. As for any hypothetical sex itself, it was "Outlook not so good," according to the Magic 8-Ball placed midway between my gut and dick.

"I don't think I ever inquired. How did you and Holger meet?"

"It was during a ski trip to Klosters in Switzerland during my junior year of college. Holger was there with some friends. Incredibly charming and accomplished on the slopes. We hit it off, and got married a year later."

"Holger's been around the track a few more times than you."

"He is eleven years older than me, yes."

"And who brought more, uh, capital to the sacred union?"

Juniper practically sprouted icicles. "I have a certain safe and sufficient income thanks to the generosity of my family. But Holger always sustained our mutual lifestyle in a very capable fashion. Right up to this unfortunate misstep."

Nothing could have been clearer to either Juniper or me: She had married a sexy Eurotrash scammer on the order of Clark Rockefeller and now was paying the price. I didn't make her say it out loud, and I refrained from any moralistic finger-pointing of my own. My moralistic fingers were too dirty and out of practice to be of much use.

"Did Holger have any offices for this cow-fart utilization thing he was putting over on people?"

"No, he worked out of his study here."

"Is it possible for me to go through his papers?"

"I suppose so—whatever the authorities left behind."

In contrast to the parlor, the study was dark and claustrophobia-inducing, with heavy velvet curtains, drawn, seeming to narrow the room to coffin size. A desk lamp with one of those useless energy-saving bulbs did little to dispel the gloom.

"Leave everything as you find it, please, and then let yourself out. I have a headache and need to lie down."

I didn't bother mentioning that this was the effect I had on all women.

At the study door, Juniper paused, and I wondered if she was going to ask me to tuck her in.

"And please don't abscond with any of the more valuable curios, if you can help yourself. Everything is under a lien, until this mess gets straightened out."

"Gotcha. My interior decorator is very picky about what I bring home to add to her designs anyway."

The Treasury men or the SEC or the IRS had plucked Holger's

files cleaner than the hotdog platter at an orphanage picnic. You could have stored the *Complete Works of Stephen King* in his desk drawers.

But by lying down on my back and looking up, I found one paper way at the rear of the bottom drawer that had been accidentally pinned, hidden, in place by the drawer above.

The letterhead read: Association of Engineering Ontologists Totalizing Affinities. An address on the outskirts of a small city upstate completed the information.

Dear Mr. Holtzclaw:

Yes, I believe AEOTA can supply your needs. But our technology is proprietary, and can only be licensed, not purchased. We would have to conduct a face-to-face meeting to discuss the exact arrangements.

Please contact us at your earliest convenience to arrange such a meeting.

Sincerely yours,
Mr. Thaumas

The date on the letter was two days before Holger had disappeared.

From Juniper's nabe to the rather seedier district where Yulia lived in the doublewide trailer I had purchased for us with the profits from reuniting an aging rock star with her daughter abandoned at birth was a journey across practically the entire socioeconomic spectrum of contemporary urban America, from upper crust to stale leftovers. Hustling seemed universal, though, no matter the income level. About the only types of citizen I did not pass during my odyssey were junkies and state legislators, although I did drive by an infamous bar where the mayor had recently been caught snorting coke in the john, so maybe I bagged two unsavory coups in one.

Yulia's usual slavically spooky sixth sense had her waiting for me glaringly in the open doorway, although I had not called. Or maybe my Nokia was secretly on her side and had texted news of my departure from Juniper's.

The Euromaidan Revolution of 2014 in the Ukraine had produced winners and losers, just like any revolution, and Yulia Lysenko had been one of the losers. Forced to abandon all her property and her job as a literature professor, due to her out-of-favor allegiances, she fled her native land to receive asylum in the USA. Her academic credentials were useless here, and she had taken a job as a bartender. The watering-hole, an upscale joint named after its owner, Joshua Greenstone, appreciated the trade brought in by the new brunette bottle-jockey's gamin good looks—though she did have what oral maxillofacial surgeons referred to as "incompetent lips." This was the condition where the normal resting state of one's face resulted in the display of teeth. Yulia looked as if she were perpetually snarling or sneering. Some guys found it really sexy, yours truly among them. Several daily tequila purchases at Joshua Greenstone's by yours truly had resulted in a date and nigh-concurrent sex.

When I could breathe and see and formulate words again after that initial bout of copulation, I said, "There is no way those are incompetent lips."

My extreme charm and wit and superhuman bedroom prowess led straight to the altar.

Our marriage lasted two-and-a-half years. Yulia quickly and correctly concluded, to her dismay, that I was eccentric, lazy, and without much ambition. But two other issues had also influenced her decision to ditch me.

The first was my propensity to mess around with other women. I can only offer the excuse that I had been a bachelor for all my adult life up until this June-October marriage, and had been set in my ways. The worst reveal of my inveterate horndoggishness occurred when Yulia had returned a day early from her reunion in Paris, France, with her mother and found the doublewide rockin'. Non-American that she was, she failed to complete and heed the advisory adage and had indeed come knockin', discovering me with a stacked naked redhead who was intent on showing me why it had been a glaring injustice to the pole-dancing profession to fire her from her job at a certain gentlemen's club, a venue that she now wanted me to bring down in revenge by highlighting various illegal practices of theirs that I could surely uncover with her athletic help.

But our short marriage might have survived such infidelities, if not for a more substantial disagreement.

And that, it turned out, underlay the immediate cause that had made Yulia summon me today.

Plainly, she had worked herself up into an indignant tizzy since our touchy but mild-mannered phone conversation of a few hours ago. She waved a piece of paper violently as I crossed the gravel walk to the trailer's wooden steps.

"Vern, this is the sickest, most vile joke you have ever played on me!"

Except in the realm of slang, Yulia's English was better than mine, but her accent surfaced during times of stress. Now she sounded like a street-market borscht vendor.

I ushered us inside and closed the door. "Calm down, Yulia. What the hell are you talking about?"

She shoved the paper under my nose.

I read the ransom note, a simple anonymous laser-print document.

YULIA RUGGLES WE HAVE YOUR DAUGHTER AEOTA
SHE WILL BE RETURNED SAFELY TO YOU FOR THE
SUM OF ONE HUNDRED THOUSAND DOLLARS
WE ARE CONFIDENT YOU AND YOUR EX HUSBAND
CAN RAISE THIS SUM OF MONEY
WHEN YOU HAVE IT READY WE WILL KNOW AND
YOU WILL RECEIVE FURTHER INSTRUCTIONS
DO NOT GO TO THE POLICE IF YOU VALUE YOUR
DAUGHTER'S LIFE

Yulia had me pinned with a look of total contempt that hurt me more than I thought she still could. So I played it for laughs.

"Not much on proper punctuation, are they?"

Tear-tracks mottling her flushed face, Yulia socked me in the chest with a small but potent fist. "You really thought this was funny? You dirty bastard!"

"Yulia, I swear, I had nothing to do with this!"

"Then why does the note use the name Aelita for our daughter? No one knows that but us!"

I looked again at the note, then turned it toward Yulia. "They don't say Aelita. They say Aeota."

Yulia knuckled her eyes, dragged a sleeve across her drippy nose, then studied the letter again. She regarded me with less hatred and more confusion.

"You're right. I thought it said Aelita . . . I guess . . . I guess I saw what I expected to see . . . "

Yulia had wanted to conceive a year after we married. Naturally, I had to reveal my ancient vasectomy. She learned the operation could often be successfully reversed. I refused. She even had a name picked out for our unborn daughter. Aelita, after some Russian movie she admired. That ongoing, vituperative disagreement was the real beginning of our end.

"Who the hell is Aeota then?"

"I don't know. I think it has something to do with this case I'm on."

Yulia grabbed the letter, crumpled it up, and threw it to the floor. "Even when we're not married I have to suffer because of your bullshit job!"

I retrieved the ransom note. "This come in an envelope?"

She found it in the trash. A plain white business-sized envelope with no writing on it. I took it nonetheless.

"I've got to go now. Call me if anything else happens that I should know about."

Outside at my car, I paused to look back.

Yulia stood in the trailer's door with her arms folded below her stomach, as if cradling what wasn't there.

4 LOCAVORE APOCALYPSE

I WAS DRIVING NORTH INTO A SHORT-LIVED killer inferno.

Well, maybe not fully into it, but close enough to get singed maybe—if I weren't careful.

Upstate was burning, several separated wildfires devouring acres of drought-dried forest and a few incidental pieces of beloved infrastructure, despite the best efforts of thousands of firefighters. Even hundreds of miles away from the living flames, the air approached Chinese-megalopolis levels of unbreathability and opacity.

Elsewhere in the nation, a couple of Katrina-wannabe storms had hit up and down the East Coast. Atlanta had experienced a freak hailstorm with celestial ice-rocks the size of Ping-Pong balls crashing down. The Midwest had seen a pack of tornadoes romping through a swath of helpless towns like teenage girls rampaging through a Wet Seal store during a 50 percent off sale. Invader species were practically climbing out of the Great Lakes to register to vote. And honeybees were dying faster than amateur comedians at open-mic night. Predictions for the upcoming winter's weather ranged from Michael Crichton direness to Book of Revelation severity.

And those were just the conditions in the USA. Of the rest of the climate-victimized world, the perp speaketh not.

There really was no denying the truth any longer: Our planet was fucked. Screwed, blued, and tattooed by humanity into a long slow death spiral. Or at least that's how it seemed to me at the moment—and to most of us, I think, when we were being honest with ourselves.

And what was to be done about the situation? Really, c'mon now, give it your best shot. Live in caves? Stop buying Big Agribiz strawberries? Carry picket signs down into coalmines? Read locally produced papyrus by candlelight instead of binge-watching TV shows? How about we just stop overbreeding like bonobos on Spring Break? Yeah, good luck with that last one. No, the average citizen, however well intentioned, had been sidelined from the playing field or benched himself on this crisis. All the low-flow showerheads you could install were not going to deliver water to these dried-out woods toward which I drove.

I was like everyone else. The only thing to do, I figured, was to keep calm and carry on. "When the world is running down, you make the best of what's still around." If humanity's bacon was ever going to be saved—a highly debatable proposition—some big-ass *deus ex machina* would have to step in, some game-changer along the lines of alien invasion, massively-lethal-only-to-humans plague, or revolutionary new technology. And neither you nor I nor my kid sister was going to play any pivotal part in those scenarios.

So I drove north, adding my share of carbon monoxide and other pollutants to the overburdened atmosphere and trying not to give a damn.

Out here in the country, without any distractions other than musing on the imminent extinction of the human race, a worn tape of Yes playing slurrily from my dashboard speakers ("Lost in losing circumstances, that's just where you are . . . "), I tried to think about this case.

Back in my office after leaving Yulia, I had packaged up the ransom note and its envelope and messengered them over to a private lab I used. I doubted I would get any fingerprints or chemical or organic signatures from the paper that would lead me anywhere, but I had to try.

After the messenger came and went—a young guy in cyclist gear, thin as my wallet—I thought about my counterfactual daughter, Aeota/Aelita. I tried to picture her unborn face. Christ, I hoped she would have favored Yulia rather than me! She'd be, what, roughly five years old by now. A real little girl. Heir and fruit of my loins. And abducted! I began to get angry for no real reason. I powered up my computer and searched for "aeota" again.

The results were radically different from the last search just a few hours ago.

The top entry on the first page, brand new, was a hit for the Association of Engineering Ontologists Totalizing Affinities, the source of the letter to Holtzclaw. I clicked over to their home page. Very glossy, lots of pictures of happy consumers enjoying themselves in various idyllic situations, indoors and out, plus dedicated employees in office and laboratory settings. Except I couldn't really identify what AEOTA did or made or traded. All I encountered was a lot of buzzwords about incentivizing and rewarding and optimizing and maximizing—and, natch, "totalizing affinities."

Back among the search results, several lines down but still on the first page, I came across another new reference.

"Aeota" had been the name of a female character in a short-lived newspaper comic strip that ran during the year 1910, Herbert

Crowley's *The Wigglemuch*. Scholar Dan Nadel had said, "For a brief period thereafter, the name received some faddish conversational usage among fans of the strip, being applied to any woman of a certain disposition, attitude, and appearance conforming to those qualities discerned in the fictional woman."

I brought up fuzzy scans of the antique strip. So far as I could tell, Aeota had been a roly-poly Polynesian, attired in native garments—that is, when she hadn't been a willowy Weimar vamp like Theda Bara, all slinky gowns, plumed tiaras, and long strands of costume beads. And did she feature a tail? Maybe I was conflating two separate characters. The eccentric lettering in the word balloons was hard to read, and the strip's plot, taking place amongst surreal creatures in a neverland, did not lend itself to casual parsing.

I took out my phone and called Marty Quartz, my go-to guy for all matters cyber.

"Vern, great to hear from you! How's the Nokia? 'That is not dead which can eternal lie, and with strange aeotas even death may die.'"

"Marty, what did you say? Strange what now?"

"Strange eons. You know the quote. Your basic Lovecraft. Hey, need a new ringtone?" Without warning, Marty blasted my ear with what sounded like two ducks shagging a coyote to death inside a galloping calliope.

"I'm honored to experience that snippet from the Arcturus Hit Parade, Marty, but I'm cool with the older ringtone you gave me. No, I need to ask you something." I recounted my before-and-after forays into the web. "How could search results change so dramatically in just a few hours?"

"The internet is a dynamic organism, Vern. It's not static, things change every second."

"Yeah, but these changes happened on the very first page of results for the same search term each time. Aren't those supposed to be the durable results with the most weight? How could something brand new instantly rise to the top?"

"Things trend, Vern. Attention drives significance and visibility. Someone else besides you must be Googling that shit and hyper-linking their brains out."

"Yeah, but these items didn't even exist in the prior search."

"Are you sure of that? Did you really study every page of the early results?"

I tried to recall if I had scrolled through every single line of the prior search. Hadn't I given up after wading through so much spam? Maybe the items about postmodern industrial AEOTA and the Herbert Crowley strip had been hiding from me just a page away.

"No, I can't be sure, Marty."

"Well, there you go. Hey, I gotta fly, Vern. I'm behind in rigging up my Burner costume. I'm going as a Red Lectroid. Hope I don't bake under all the latex prosthetics."

As the line went unceremoniously dead, I realized I had not asked him about the way my phone had disgorged a printed slip of paper.

As I was re-pocketing my Nokia, the same bike messenger guy returned. No way the lab could have turned around my assignment so fast.

But it was just a coincidence. The kid was delivering a package to me, a small item wrapped in kraft paper, no trace of sender.

Somebody obviously thought it was Christmas and I had been a very good little boy.

Nestled in cotton batting in an unmarked cardboard jeweler's box, smaller than the one delivered to me by Brevis Baxter, was a cheap charm bracelet with only four cheap pewter charms on it:

a magnifying glass, a gift-wrapped present, a page-a-day calendar and a representation of the Milky Way as seen from above, a spiral-armed whirlpool.

find aeota yesterday everywhere.

I tore the box and kraft paper apart, looking for a note or a clue, but came up dry.

Now I was getting a little pissed-off. Two mysterious deliveries in one day. That pegged the private-eye suspiciousness meter to the max.

I dropped the charm bracelet in the same pocket that held the slip of paper that my phone had spat out, then went down to my car.

I knew I was going to have to visit AEOTA in person . . .

Now the GPS showed I was only about half an hour away from my destination. Rural scenery still predominated, a dozen shades of brown with here and there some besieged green. I came abreast of a neatly tended farm amidst a manifestly irrigated cornfield with a big barn bearing an old-school advertisement painted right on the planks of its roadside wall.

I slammed on the brakes, shifted, and zoomed back in reverse, heedless of traffic conditions behind me. Luckily, the lone car coming saw my crazy actions in time to swerve with a blast of horn.

I found the driveway to the farm and pulled in.

Standing a few feet from the barn wall, I verified I had not imagined the sight.

CHEW AEOTA PLUG

FOR DISCERNING MEN OF SUPERIOR TASTE

NO FINER FLAVOR NOR GRAIN

"ALL THE CHORUS AEOLIAN

"SINGS ITS PRAISE IN AEOTA LAND"

I pondered the drawing of the tobacco pouch: the trademark featured a kind of pre-nubile vestal virgin wrapped in a flowing robe and holding up a single big tobacco leaf with both hands. Real *Little Nemo* look.

Even in the smoky gloom of the forest fire–tinged atmosphere, the colors on the sign were, if vintage, inexplicably hardly faded.

"Pretty awesome, am I right?"

I turned to confront a young couple, obviously the farm's owners. The round-faced woman was black and displayed her hair in a kind of upgathered pineapple-foliage fountain. She wore rubber boots and carried a murmuring buff-colored chicken big as a hypertrophied turkey. Her white male partner had on dirty bib overalls and sported a beard thick as the barbed wire around a refugee camp. Grow-local hipsters, "American Gothic" for the Whole Foods era. They were both smiling.

"We redid the barn last year," said the guy. "Stripped off all the old siding, and there she was. Protected from the elements for about ninety years."

"What do you know about the history of that brand? Anything?"

The man took out his cellphone and tip-tap-flick-swiped up a screen of thumbnail images. "Oh, sure. Lots of information on the web. It's not made anymore though. Company went out of business around 1970. So we adopted the name for our farm."

I stared at the guy's screen, seeing the Aeota tobacco pouch replicated in a dozen era-variant styles. I knew that when I returned to my office, I'd find the same data showing on my screen, where it had never appeared before in previous searches.

"Well, thanks. I gotta go now."

"Take a dozen eggs," offered the woman pleasantly. "We've got more than we can sell."

Behind the wheel again, I cast frequent sidelong glances at the carton of Aeota Farm eggs on the passenger seat. The hipsters had shopped the image of the vestal virgin out of context and replaced the tobacco leaf in her hands with an uplofted, much-larger-than-life egg.

5 Judge Dread

THE OPALESCENT MURK OUTSIDE MY WINDSHIELD
had gotten pretty bad by the time I hit the outskirts of the city where
AEOTA had its corporate HQ, and I was grateful I didn't have to
head any further north. Just breathing this stuff was becoming
problematical.

Past an elementary school, a mall, a junkyard, a milk-bottling
plant—

find aeota yesterday everywhere.

The building that housed AEOTA bore discreet signage in a
modest font attesting to the company's humble presence. An elegant
single-story block of offices, more viridian-tinted glass than steel,
was dwarfed by a tall windowless monolithic manufactory wing
longer than a couple of football fields, all utilitarian coppery metal.

I took a visitor's parking space and entered a pleasant atrium. A
receptionist ensconced as eye-candy behind a circular desk might
have wandered in off the pages of *Vanity Fair* magazine.

"I'd like to see Mr. Thaumas, please."

"You're expected?"

"No. But if you tell him I want to talk about Holger Holtzclaw and
Eurybia Enterprises, he might get all puppy-dog eager."

Three minutes later, I had a temporary badge and a guide—a young intern who looked as if he could shave the down from his cheeks with a lettuce leaf—and was heading toward what I hoped were, if not some definitive answers, at least some further milestones along this crazy road. I felt a little as if I were Nick Fury walking through the dangerous corridors of AIM, but since I didn't see any guys in yellow bee-keeper suits, I tried to shrug off the feeling. Besides, I wasn't right for the role of Nick: I looked awful with an eyepatch.

The wooden door bore the title of CEO and my man's full name: Thomas T. Thaumas.

I don't know who I expected to see behind that door. The Devil, Gordon Gekko, Hannibal Lecter, Dr. Evil. But whatever menacing figure my imagination might have supplied, it wasn't that of Judge Hardy.

Old cultural touchstones evaporate, exhibiting a half-life determined by a complex formula involving nursing-home mortality stats and the ratings of certain nostalgia-driven cable channels. Once upon a time, everyone knew the Andy Hardy movies. Mickey Rooney as the boy who defined the then-newly minted modern teenager. Familiar enough to inspire a thousand imitations and parodies. And Andy's dad, played by actor Lewis Stone, almost as familiar. Wispy white hair receding from a high, intelligent dome of a forehead. Strong, elderly-handsome craggy face, more long than square. Clear, dispassionate, ironic gaze—stern but fair. Always dressed in plain dark tasteful suits and vest, with one of those floppy ties seen mostly on Golden Age comic book senators of yore.

That proved to be Thomas T. Thaumas to a T. Except for the Blue-tooth headset that Judge Hardy had never envisioned.

The door shut of its own volition behind me as I crossed the oxblood-colored carpet. I had just enough time to quickly take in burl-wood walls adorned with soothing abstract paintings and a large window looking out over a grassy courtyard where AEOTANS strolled and lunched, before I confronted the CEO of AEOTA.

Thaumas wheeled out from behind his desk, a sculpted, bare-topped mass all stainless steel, birch, and walnut in aerodynamic lines. He compensated for his stick-like legs, which barely bulked out his trousers, with one of those hi-tech wheelchairs that could climb stairs and elevate the sitter to eye-level in cherry-picker fashion. Simultaneously heightening himself as he moved forward, he produced a disorienting sensation in my brain, as if several dimensions of the universe were involuting.

Neither smiling nor frowning, utterly neutral and businesslike, Thaumas extended a hand and we shook. I wasn't invited to sit, and indeed there were no spare chairs.

"Mr. Ruggles, your inquiry, conveyed to our receptionist, concerned a potential past client of ours, one Holger Holtzclaw. What is it you wish to know about our dealings?"

"He received a letter from your firm just a day or two before he disappeared, suggesting that he should visit you. Did he ever keep that appointment? If he did, then your firm was one of his last known contacts. His wife and creditors are eager to track him down, and they have hired me for the job."

"Mr. Holtzclaw did indeed visit us recently. I can get you the exact date and time if you need it. But after a tour of our facilities, he learned that our technology was unsuitable for his needs, and we parted ways permanently, with no subsequent contact or open channels. I'm afraid I have no idea of his current whereabouts."

"What was he after? What made your tech not useful to him?"

"Mr. Holtzclaw was interested in capturing and sequestering

31

methane from landfills. Our own processes actually generate methane, the exact opposite of what he needed. I am afraid he learned of us through secondhand information, and misunderstood the nature of our work."

"What exactly is the nature of AEOTA's mission, Mr. Thaumas? I haven't been able to figure that out yet myself."

Thaumas pinned me with a glacial granitic gaze, and I felt like young Andy summoned onto the carpet for playing hooky, or knocking up Judy Garland.

"Our firm pursues many disciplines, Mr. Ruggles, some with obvious synergies and others that might seem, to the uninitiated, to be utterly divergent. We sponsor R&D programs in a variety of areas. But our overriding ethos and raison d'être is plainly on display in our name. We believe that reality can be shaped by skilled intentions. That's ontological engineering. The noosphere or realm of human thought governs all that is. We apply the shaping precepts we have deduced and mastered, and reality changes to match our dictates."

"Are you talking about introducing new ideas and products and technologies into the world, and then hoping they are used as you intend? Shaping the culture that way, like Microsoft or Google or Monsanto? Or are you pumping me full of New Age woo-woo?"

Thaumas allowed himself the smallest of smiles. "Perhaps both, Mr. Ruggles."

"And what the hell is 'totalizing affinities?'"

"It's as the poet famously ordained, Mr. Ruggles: 'Only connect.' We identify affinities, both overt and covert, explicit and implicit, then work to totalize them, to both utterly comprehend these secret connections and to foster their interlocking syzygy."

"Well, to be perfectly frank, Mr. Thaumas, all this sounds like a truckload of mystical, investor-befuddling bullshit to me. But so long as your stockholders are happy, who am I to quibble?"

"You are entitled to your opinion of course, Mr. Ruggles."

"Do you think I can see whatever it was you showed Holtzclaw?"

"But of course, Mr. Ruggles. You need only sign a simple non-disclosure agreement consisting of a single paragraph." Thaumas activated his headset mic. "Ms. Bagasse, would you please bring in a copy of the standard visitor's NDA? And please summon Dr. Ponto to conduct a tour."

A pretty young assistant whose perfume alone had to count as some kind of perk for the executives she worked with came swiftly. I read and signed the form. While we waited for my guide, I said, "What's the T stand for?"

It seemed to me that Thaumas only pretended not to comprehend. "What T would that be, Mr. Ruggles?"

"Your middle initial."

"It stands for Totenwelt. It's an old family name. It refers to the land of the spirits, the dead, the fey. My female ancestors were all witches, you see."

6 A Visit with Microbial Matt

Before I could reply to Thaumas's somewhat unsettling familial disclosure, Dr. Matt Ponto arrived.

To say I was kinda taken aback by his appearance would be akin to claiming that the fussy old maid had been nonplussed by the nextdoor backyard orgy.

For a moment, I thought I had fallen into Middle-earth, or at least the Peter Jackson stage set thereof. Ponto was a bandy-legged dwarf, heavily muscled, a fact easy to discern from his arm-and-leg-revealing outfit of green cargo shorts and Hawaiian shirt printed with a photorealistic nebula. He wore thick-soled hiking sandals. A shaggy mane of blond hair crested above his eyes and a thick golden beard began more or less just under them, leaving him peering out as if from a military bunker's slit.

He grabbed my hand and squeezed it like a garlic press deals with a ripe clove. A kind of bumbling bonhomie radiated off him. His voice was surprisingly high, at odds with the rest of him. "You're Vern, right? Bagasse told me on the way in. Call me Microbial Matt. Everyone does. My specialty. Bugs of all sorts. But it's a pun too on my big project. I don't know if pun is the right word, exactly. You'll see. C'mon, let's go, the day's not getting any younger."

Ponto grabbed my left arm just above the elbow in a nerve-damaging pinch that brooked no resistance and steered me out the door. What was it with strangers today feeling free to make use of my bod? I looked over my shoulder to say goodbye to Thaumas, but he had already swiveled his chair and was motoring back behind his desk, lowering his seat at the same time. The combined movements provided the sensation that he was shrinking, disappearing down some converging set of lines that led to a vanishing point in a surrealist canvas.

Ponto led me through a cube farm where no one bothered to look up to the rear of the office wing, then carded us through a locked door and into the huge windowless structure behind the façade. I expected to immediately enter a facility like NASA's famed Vehicle Assembly Building. But just beyond the entrance was only a many-doored corridor of modest dimensions, not the cavernous warehouse I had half-expected.

"Labs and stuff here, but you don't want to see that. Boring, innocuous. No, you want to see Vaalbara. That's what I showed Holtzclaw. He found it fascinating. Didn't want to leave! But first we have to get you kitted out. Otherwise you wouldn't last too long. No, you definitely need to be able to breathe to enjoy Vaalbara."

I don't think I had even said so much as hello since Ponto had taken charge. Trying to shift the conversation or slow down our pace was the same frustrating and impossible task that Bugs Bunny faced every time Taz came on the scene.

Ponto brought us to a kind of locker room. I did a double-take. Hanging on pegs were several lime-green suits with boots and hoods attached that did indeed resemble the outfits of AIM.

"Powered Respirator Protective Suit," Ponto explained. "PRPS. We call them perps. Get dressed. Oh, ditch any metal, too."

7 "A Title on the Door Deserves a Vaalbara on the Floor"

I EXPECTED SOMETHING OUT OF THE ORDINARY when, after discarding my phone and keys and other metallic objects on a shelf, including that mysterious charm bracelet, Ponto and I had to cycle through an airlock to see what he wanted to show me. Gasketed outer door dogged tight. The hiss, muffled by my beekeeper headgear, of pumped-out air, leaving us in partial vacuum. I sent out silent thanks to the quality-control staff at the PRPS factory. Then an equivalent hiss of new atmosphere arriving. Finally, the rubber-buffered inner door unlatched. And on the far side—

We had stepped out onto a small railless lanai or platform that projected out, midway up a wall, over a high-roofed expanse of seemingly empty "factory" floor that must've been equivalent to about a dozen football fields in dimensions of six by two. The illumination inside this vast space was weird—like outdoor sunlight, but considerably less bright than noon of a cloudless day, and also with uncanny spectral differences I couldn't quite pin down.

Sudden slow and weighty ripplings twelve feet below the platform forced a realization upon me. What I had taken for a flat featureless floor was really the top layer of an enormous tank full of—something. From the nature of its movements, I surmised that the slinkily undulant material, a glabrous blue-green shot through with streaks of gray and opal, formed a seamless blanket atop millions of gallons of unknown fluid.

I turned to Ponto, and his voice reached me via speakers built into the hood of my perps.

"The light mimics what we understand to have been the unprocessed sunlight of the Archean Eon, some four billion years ago. Seventy percent of our current luminosity, with more UV. Our young sun was lazy and liked to spit. Vaalbara was a supercontinent of that era, hence the code name."

"And the floating carpet is—?"

Ponto grinned big behind his plastic faceplate. "That's LUCA."

"You named this stuff after a Suzanne Vega song?"

Ponto promptly pish-poshed my ignorance. "Last universal common ancestor. The rudimentary firstborn Terran, and mother of all subsequent life on the planet."

"And you found this living fossil where?"

"We didn't find it. We reverse engineered it from many different extant organisms, including the methanogens in your gut. *Methanobrevibacter smithii* and its cousins."

"So it's just a simulation of the original."

"If you insist. But we think it's pretty darn close to identical. That makes it an emulation, which is qualitatively superior to a mere simulation."

"You say 'Franken-STEIN' and I say 'Franken-STEEN.' How come the airlock?"

"LUCA is an anoxic methanogen. Oxygen would kill it, and it pumps out methane as a byproduct of its metabolism. That's why you couldn't bring in any metal that could strike a spark and set the whole atmosphere off. Can you imagine the results? Even the electric lighting units are behind transparent barriers."

"What's in the tank?"

"An emulation of the Archean ocean. Different pH, higher salinity, different dissolved mineral mix. We had to measure analogous existing African alkaline lakes with Laser Ablation Inductively Coupled Plasma Mass Spectrometry to learn—"

"T.M.I., Matt. T.M.I. Just answer one last question, though. What's it for?"

"What is life for, Vern? LUCA is its own reason for existing."

"Don't bullshit me, kid. Nobody invests hundreds of millions in research and infrastructure and daily maintenance on something that has no payout. What's AEOTA's stake in this? What's their intent?"

Ponto's face registered genuine dismay and sadness. "Can't you believe in discovering knowledge just for its own sake, Vern? We do, here at AEOTA."

I gazed out over the Sargasso of purposeless flatulent crud. The odd light and the unvarying expanse, as well as the hypnotic small oscillating and spreading quivers of LUCA's bulk, began to have a disorienting effect on me. The walls of the space seemed to swell and bulge and pulse before they receded, eventually disappearing entirely, while the carpet of LUCA spread to fill the new vacancy. The roof evaporated, revealing the low-intensity Archean sun. The limit of my new vision was the far horizon of the planet, a globe entirely covered in this slime. And I—I was standing on the prow of a ship I couldn't see, moving slowly on an endless voyage across the unchanging monoculture.

I felt myself getting dizzy. I began to sway a little.

Ponto's gloved hand on my shrouded shoulder brought me back to the present reality.

"You feeling okay, Vern? Maybe you should put your head between your knees."

"That's for nosebleeds . . . " I started to say.

And then Ponto's reassuring hand slipped down my back, was joined by its sturdy gloved mate, and despite my assailant's dwarfish stature, those two traitorous mitts managed to shove me off my feet and over the edge of the slab.

8 ROLL OUT THE WELCOME MAT

THE FALL TOOK AN ETERNITY. I SEEMED TO plummet for days. I had time to anticipate my landing, plan my escape from the Vaalbara room, and plot and carry out my elaborate revenge on Microbial Matt, Thomas T. Thaumas, and the entire human resources flowchart of AEOTA, including that pretty administrative assistant who smelled so classy. But all my rational forecasts were to prove useless.

I hit the surface of LUCA like a Hollywood stunt man hitting an air mattress, nice and cushioned. I bounced twice in a low arc, then thrice, finally coming to a rest totally unharmed, so far as I could tell. That I did not pierce the surface and fall through to the Archean sea was likewise welcome.

But something was still wrong. It took me a few seconds before I realized what.

I could smell an odor other than my own fear-sweat and booze-breath.

I could smell the sea, this particular ancient sea and whatever vegetal musk its lone citizen contributed. I expected also some kind of rotten-egg smell from LUCA's farts. But then I remembered that methane was scentless, and the typical sewer-gas smells we all recognized came from other chemical components that must have been absent here. It dawned on me that the pong was identical to the odor that had wafted from the box of sludge that Brevis Baxter had given me in the bar earlier today.

The fall must have split a seam in my perps.

Whatever the original capacity and duration of my air supply, it was now compromised by the invading methane atmosphere. Suddenly I felt—or imagined I felt—a scratchiness in my throat.

I had to move fast.

I flipped off my back and got into a hands-and-knees posture. From that position, I tried to stand. But the wavering, flexible membrane that was LUCA kept knocking me off my pins. It was worse than trying to remain upright in a bounce house full of birthday-cake-sugared-up kids.

In the few seconds of verticality I achieved on each attempt before toppling over, I managed to discern that the viewing platform was now empty of anyone, and the door back into the AEOTA HQ was shut. I also noted with relief that there was a ladder bolted to the wall, leading up from LUCA—actually, presumably, from the level of the underwater floor—and to the lanai.

I realized belatedly, like the panicky dimwit that I was, that I didn't actually need to stand. I could crawl to the ladder, which was only a few yards away, thanks to my initial small bouncing arcs. So I started to crab across the living carpet, my eyes fixed on the reassuring nearby solid wall of the chamber.

I was making good progress, I thought, when I suddenly found myself crawling *downward*, as if into a pit.

And that's exactly what was happening.

Without ripping open, LUCA was forming a depression beneath me, either voluntarily or instinctively, or perhaps due to some structural defect in this section.

I tried to scrabble faster, up the far slope of the ditch, but it kept getting deeper faster than I could advance.

Soon my weight was pulling in the pit's rim like a drawstring closing a pouch. I was being invaginated, trapped in a vacuole like an invader in a cell's defenses.

Darkness. I was now entirely encapsulated. The walls contracted close about me.

And then my suit began to melt. I didn't feel any burning where my street clothes exposed my skin—just a slippery wetness, as when a dog slobbers on you.

I tried to hold my breath. But I could only last so long. I had to suck in lungsful of the mock-Archean air. The warm antediluvian, unoxygenated stuff filled my lungs, and immediately I could feel my thoughts begin to spin out of my control. Hallucinatory waves of random spinning objects began to invade my inner vision, and sheets of color like the aurora borealis came and went.

Before I dived fully under the chaos, I managed to formulate one last rational deduction:

This was how Holger Holtzclaw disappeared.

But I couldn't figure out how I was going to get back to tell his wife Juniper and collect my fee.

9 INTERVIEW WITH AN ANCESTOR

I WAS FLOATING HIGH ABOVE A PLANET, presumably Earth. Not quite far away enough to see an entire hemisphere, but plenty high enough. And my view was unlike any aerial shot of Earth that I had ever seen before. That was because the entire surface of this globe was molten, all orange and ruby and charcoal, like a flaming pizza fresh from God's own wood-fired oven. Incandescent magma flowed like unholy dark kombucha at a vegan retreat, with frequent great geysers and gouts and gushes of it exploding skyward in lacy traceries, causing me to flinch every time, although whatever form I currently occupied seemed distant enough to be immune to these outbursts.

After some indefinite period of observation I realized with uncanny certainty that I was looking at Hadean Earth, our world as it had existed over four-and-a-half billion years ago, raw and still forming. The awesome majesty of the spectacle, unseen by any human before me, left me suitably humbled and stunned. The only thing missing to complete the numinous experience was a Stokowski-conducted *Rites of Spring* playing in the background, followed by some romping Disney dinosaurs.

The next five hundred million years passed both slowly and

quickly. I seemed to be aware of every creeping second, and yet at the same time, eons flicked by in less time than an eyeblink. I don't ever recall feeling bored. I don't think I was driven insane. At the same time, I gained no infinite wisdom, no particularly brilliant insights into my condition or the human condition in general. Instead, I just existed heedlessly and unconcernedly in some kind of thought-free fugue state.

And eventually, when changing circumstances on the planet below jogged me out of my semi-aware, semi-blank hibernation, I awoke as the same old Vern Ruggles, PI, that I had been before all this began, just as ham-handed, flummoxed, day-late-and-a-dollar short as ever, proving again the sagacity of several old adages like "pearls before swine" and "you can lead a whore to culture, but you can't make her think."

Below me the Earth had gone relatively cool and quiescent, its rocky face solidified into convoluted young bare mountains and valleys and unadorned plains. Long rains had come and gone, running in rivers down to naked shores, and oceans empty of substance prevailed.

Suddenly, on one corner of the eternal seas, a spot of familiar color bloomed. The unlikely glitch of life had happened, bootstrap miracle. LUCA. In a span of subjective seconds, an interval really representing many millions of years, the little patch spread until all the waters were curtained with the living mat.

At that point I began somehow, volitionlessly, to descend. There was no sensation of wind or heat from my rapid passage, just the transition of my mind's eye, down, down, down—until I was standing, newly embodied, on the gently heaving trampoline of LUCA.

I lifted an arm and hand that I was surprised to possess. I tilted and swiveled my head in the usual manner, a sensation now fresh and novel, taking in my familiar naked body. I kicked at the vegetal raft and could feel the squishy resistance and rebound. The immature sun coated my skin with solar comfort, and a sudden flash downpour left me sodden. But the tropical warmth, remnant of the Hadean days, soon evaporated the moisture.

All in all, if I had to be stuck back in the Archean I would have preferred to remain a disembodied watcher. Existence was going to get awfully boring awfully fast, as the only sentient inhabitant of an entire world. That is, assuming I could survive here for any length of time. There was plenty of potable water, to be sure. But what was I going to eat, other than LUCA? I sat down cross-legged on the damp carpet. Should I sample a piece now? Better to find out sooner rather than later whether I was going to starve to death. I wondered what the stuff would taste like, and whether eating one's Last Universal Common Ancestor would count as cannibalism of the most esoteric sort.

Curiously, I did not even bother to ponder how I had time-traveled four-and-a-half billion years backwards from the Vaalbara room at AEOTA. It seemed futile to waste any time speculating, since what mattered was the undeniable fact of my presence here.

I dug the fingers of my right hand into the mat and strained at the interwoven strands, which resisted my pull more strongly than I had anticipated. "Give it up, you mother!" The sound of my own voice shocked me, after almost a billion years of silence.

But the shock was nothing compared to the sensation of hearing another voice.

"Stop that, please. It is unpleasant."

I froze. The calm, mellifluous voice had come from behind me. Very slowly I maneuvered from my butt to my hands and knees, keeping my eyes fixed on the "floor."

45

When I raised my face, I found I was looking almost into the pellucid aquamarine eyes of a standing human female child, whose pale Caucasian face was just a bit higher than mine. Naked, the kid appeared to be about four or five years old—my best guess, since I'm no expert on rug rats. The lines of her juvenile countenance were disturbingly familiar and yet, simultaneously, utterly unknown.

"Who are you?"

"I'm your daughter, Aelita."

As she pronounced her name, I heard the phonemes of it curiously doubled. It sounded like a smeared overlay of "Aelita" and "Aeota," with neither one predominating, almost as if you had multi-tracked the same voice saying the different names at the same decibel level.

I studied the little girl's charming and pleasant features for a while. Placid and unhurried, she submitted to my inspection. I thought that maybe I could fancifully discern a blend of my genes and Yulia's. But then I noticed the dead giveaway showing the truth of her identity.

The kid had incompetent lips. With all the muscles of her face serenely relaxed, her front teeth still showed.

"Oooh . . . kay. Pleased to meet you. Though I thought that based on our supposed relationship we would have popped up on each other's Facebook timelines long before now."

"Why don't you stand up? I prefer to walk while we discuss things."

Of course, her tone and diction and vocabulary resembled no five-year-old's ever. "Is this a sight-seeing tour? Because judging by what I observed from on high, one spot on this fuzzy green liquid tennis ball is pretty much like any other. Or are we going to a restaurant somewhere? Tell me it's a restaurant, please. I haven't had a bite to eat since the Hadean, and that was one billion o'clock ago."

Aelita smiled, and extended her hand. I managed to stand up on the mat of LUCA, which seemed less roiling than its counterpart back in my era. I took her small warm hand in mine and we began to stroll. Technically, I guess, we were walking on water.

"Do you like this world?"

"It's all right, I suppose. Not a lot of variety. 'I miss the honky-tonks, Dairy Queens, and 7-Elevens,' if you know what I mean."

"I agree. This phase of life was an essential and invaluable foundation. But it had to change. The gradient of biotic complexity and its strange attractors demanded it."

"Uh, yeah, just what I was going to say."

Aelita remained silent for some time. I thought for a moment that I should be freaking out at my lack of clothes and her toddler nakedness. But actually, I realized, it felt totally natural and pure in this isolated remove from all of society's hang-ups.

"Would you want this state to prevail again in your time?"

"What? No! Of course not!"

"But someone does."

"Who? Thaumas and company?"

"Yes, they are players. But behind them and their allies stands another. He resides as far from your era into futurity as we stand now in the past. His name is DUCA. Descendant Ultimately Converged from All."

"And this DUCA thingy wants to do—what?"

"He wants to remake all the eons between him and your time so as to extend his realm of sameness ever further backwards, beyond its accorded origins."

"Let me get this straight. DUCA wants to undo four billion years of history between his time and mine?"

"Yes. But more than that. He wants to undo the same interval between your time and this era, until he and LUCA can meet and merge. His lust is bent toward only this."

"So if he succeeds, there'd be no history to Earth except for eight billion years of horny kelp?"

"Yes, that is correct."

"Holy fucking Christ."

"I need your help to stop DUCA and make it impossible for all time for him to succeed."

"My help? What the hell can I do? And why me?"

"I cannot show you the answers to those questions. You have to learn from the Green Lady."

"Aw, no, c'mon now! No more freaky strangers, okay?"

"Farewell. I will see you again soon."

"Aelita, wait!"

But my kid wasn't much on filial obedience. She touched me, and I was gone.

10 INTERVIEW WITH A VENUSIAN

AT FIRST I THOUGHT NOTHING HAD CHANGED upon Aelita's proclamation that I was off to see some other wizard. Although the unsettling little girl had vanished, I was still floating naked on a topsy-turvy vegetal raft under a bright sun. But then the differences hit me.

The sun was bigger and whiter and hotter than the Archean luminary. And the plant life island beneath me was just that: an isolated territory with definite boundaries, at least one edge of which I could see, not part of a universal mat. Moreover, its denser bulk supported elaborate vegetation, trees and bushes and grass-like stuff. The trees featured purple trunks and orange foliage, causing me to reach up to the crown of my head to feel if I was suddenly sporting a Seussian topknot like a Sneetch. But no such luck. And animals! Something very much like a small dragon. I backed away nervously, but the creature ignored me, and began calmly eating a fallen yellow fruit round as a toy balloon.

All of this was vaguely, disturbingly half-familiar to me. I racked my brain for any past acquaintance with such a landscape. A Roger Dean album cover? *Tales from the Topographic Ocean*? Some scene from *Avatar*? And then it hit me.

49

This was Perelandra, C. S. Lewis's impossible watery Venus. I had read the book and its companions in college, though I retained only hazy memories of the whole trilogy, thanks to an accompanying haze of dope smoke. And, upon realizing the nature of this place, another revelation hit me.

I was not here physically. I was hallucinating all this. The fact that I was now occupying a fictional world stored in the unattended shelves of my subconscious was the tipoff. My environment was all the sputtering collage hastily assembled by my evaporating neurons, a real Ambrose-Bierce, Owl-Creek-Bridge trip. In reality, I was dying or already dead back in the Vaalbara room at AEOTA HQ. My perps suit had burst upon my fall, and I was breathing in the pure methane atmosphere, suffocating. Matt Ponto was already getting ready to dispose of the offloaded contents of my pockets—my Nokia, the mysterious charm bracelet, my wallet holding thirty-five dollars and an autographed publicity photo of Uma Thurman as Poison Ivy—in some oubliette, then drive my car off a cliff, all to throw the authorities off my track when I was reported missing. Goodbye, Vern Ruggles, PI.

Yes, this had to be the case. It was a much simpler answer than believing I had been transported back five billion years in time by LUCA, or that I was now resident on an imaginary Venus that modern science utterly denied.

This new belief—that all this was a deathbed phantasm—was surprisingly welcome and reassuring, liberating in fact. Dying or dead, I had no more responsibilities. My actions, such as they were, were meaningless. I could just sit back and enjoy the ride, for as long as it lasted.

"Man of Thulcandra, your cogitations are awry."

I jumped at the voice. Jesus, why were women always sneaking up on me lately?

Turning, I saw just whom I had expected to see: Tinidril, the Green Lady of Venus, one of only two people on the entire planet. And she was a total babe, with curves that made the Riviera's Grande Corniche look like the Bonneville Salt Flats.

"Are you in my head? Oh, pardon me. What a foolish question. You're *out* of my head!"

Tinidril's smile was simultaneously pitying and appreciative. "You jest in a sophisticated fashion. But there is no truth to your delusions. This world is as real as the one you come from, and you are here in body as well as spirit. If you do not believe me, then take my hand."

Why not play along? I stepped forward willingly. "Listen, doll—if my mind can conjure up this whole crazy-ass landscape and make it seem solid and tangible to me, then it should have no problem making me think I'm holding some dame's hand."

Tinidril said nothing, but merely continued to smile and extend her delicate leaf-colored hand. So I grabbed it.

My surroundings vanished as an electric current seemed to pump through me. I was hovering bodiless in space again, this time somewhere out around the Asteroid Belt, seeing Mars and Venus and Earth as exotically hued spheres out of all proper proportions to each other. And I also saw the attendant deities, the *eldila*, giant columns of wavering light, one for each planet. But the one for Earth was somehow tainted, evil. I recalled that this was the "dark archon" who made life on Earth so hellish.

The dark archon seemed somehow to sense me, and turn its faceless attention in my direction. I could feel waves of hatred and anger emanating toward me from it. I tried to flee, but got nowhere, as the mad deity raced closer, and closer—

Tinidril had released my hand, and I was back on the Perelandra raft, sweating and shaking.

"Jesus, Mary, and Joseph! Was that strictly necessary?"

"You had to apprehend the threat we face. Call him the Bent One, or DUCA, the danger is the same. He will unmake your world's proper destiny. You must strive with all your powers to thwart this."

"But why me?"

"Be not afeared. You are not alone in this mission. There are others. But why any individual is chosen lies beyond my comprehension, and yours."

"So what do I have to do?"

"You will be returned to Thulcandra, where matters will reveal themselves in good order. Respond to each circumstance as it arises. Just be brave, confident and serene."

"You don't happen to have a prescription handy for that, do you?"

Tinidril grinned. "Yes, actually, I do."

She pushed and tripped me all at once, and I went onto my back. Then she was straddling me, her fleshy weight as real as anything I had ever felt, and I had an instant aching boner like the mainmast of a visiting Tall Ship. She reached between her legs and guided my dick up her slippery moss-tufted hole. If holding her hand had been enlightening, then her robust rocking upon my cock was satori squared.

"Ransome," she called out. "My Ransome!"

The ransom note Yulia had showed me popped into my oscillating brain.

And then my nova of an orgasm brought instant oblivion.

11 Waking Up High and Dry

I wasn't lying on the LUCA trampoline in the Archean period, nor on a Venusian floating green acre. And I wasn't naked, with a hard-riding Green Lady atop me.

Instead, I was recumbent on a hard gritty concrete floor, wearing the same tatty outfit of jeans and faded polo shirt and boat shoes that I had been wearing when I made that drive through the forest-fire-smoke-thronged precincts of my state—a journey that seemed to me now both infinitely remote and impossibly recent.

The hard gritty concrete floor of the totally empty Vaalbara room at AEOTA HQ.

For a minute or so I did not move, just trying to take in the meaning of my surroundings, feeling whiplashed from all the transitions I had undergone. My limited slice of vision showed me the wall that hosted the viewing platform from which I had been pushed, and the adjacent ladder. I could also admire some of the roof of the building, which was gaping with ragged holes through which a brilliant blue sky showed.

Finally I mustered enough energy and gumption to stand up and look all around.

The enormous hangar-like space was completely vacant. No

surrogate ancient ocean, no floating carpet of Last Universal Common Ancestor. The place smelled like a distillation of Medieval cathedral and old person's coat closet, with a grace note of outside breezes courtesy of the roof holes. Old fixtures on the floor showed where machinery had been bolted.

I began to walk toward the ladder, my footsteps echoing, my legs unsteady, as if anticipating bobbing, rocking motions that weren't there. At the base of the ladder, I noticed the metal rungs were flaked with rust. But they seemed strong enough to support me, so up I went.

On the lanai, I found the airlock door ajar. I pulled it further open, and noted its hinges stiff with disuse. I passed through, and out the second gasketed door.

The last time I had stood here—billions of years ago, or just hours ago, or some intermediary interval—the room on the far side of the airlock had held an array of PRPS gear. Now the racks were empty of suits, and in fact seemed disproportionate for any such gear. Discarded scraps of paper littered the floor.

Without much hope, I went to the locker where I had stored, as instructed, all my spark-producing metal gear: enigmatic charm bracelet, Nokia, car keys, etc.

Inside was a dusty gift box of Old Sandstone booze. I picked up the box: too light to hold a bottle, full or empty. Too bad; I could've really used a slug. I shook it. Several objects jostled about inside. I peeled back the box flaps, and emptied out my possessions, all seemingly none the worse for whatever passage of time they had experienced. I tossed the box to the floor.

I pocketed everything but the phone, then powered up my Nokia and it caught a signal right away. My fingers hesitated over the keypad. Who could I call in such a situation? No one, really. Best to get back to my office and see what developed from there. Size up the situation, do a recon, assess the evidence, try to figure out just what the hell had happened while I was passed out or time-traveling or space-traveling or hallucinating or whatever the Christ I had been doing since Matt Ponto pushed me off that platform.

Before I could put away my phone, a text arrived.

```
destroy aeota tomorrow everywhere.
```

This was followed by the same question my phone had asked me earlier:

```
PRINT TEXT Y/N?
```

Selecting Y produced another strip of paper out the magic printer slit in the top of the phone. Again, four emojis. Three were the same, but the first was different, a kind of firecracker bang.

I stuck the paper in my pants pocket, where I had stashed its earlier counterpart.

The rest of AEOTA HQ was just as unused, dusty, trashed, detritus-strewn, and empty of clues as the Vaalbara room had been. If I were to trust what I saw, the place had been untenanted for at least a couple of years, if not longer.

Had my time-jaunt been imprecise? Maybe I had been returned to some year in advance of when I had left. Or maybe I had slept, Rip Van Winkle style, beneath the surface of the artificial ocean after my plummet and invagination, miraculously preserved in some kind of shell of stasis, until the whole abandoned tank drained away and I awoke.

I figured that I would discover which answer best suited the reality once I got back to the city.

Exiting the building, I turned to look back at its façade.

A huge dilapidated sign on a metal framework atop the roof proclaimed:

AEOTA CANDY COMPANY

MAKERS OF FAMOUS HADES FIREBALLS

I had never heard of that candy, and I was pretty sure no such firm had shown up in my internet search.

My car was parked right near the exit. Unlike the building, it showed no sign of time's passage, no coating of grime nor cloak of fallen leaves. The disparity was puzzling. It was as if when I had arrived, this building had already been in its current condition.

I laid my hand on the hood of my car. The engine was still warm.

I slung my ass into the driver's seat, and my old beater started right up. The engine certainly did not sound as if it had been sitting here inactive for a year or more.

The trip back to the city revealed nothing amiss. There were no mutants or aliens or undead zombies roaming the landscape, no unprecedented skyscrapers connected by aerial bridges, no giant visor-helmeted robot standing watch beside a flying saucer. Just the usual traffic and mundane sights.

I went straight to my office, rather than to my crummy divorcee's apartment. Everything normal, so far as I could tell. Seated, I dug out the bottle of tequila, its level unchanged from when I had last poured it "a few hours ago." I downed a hit straight from the bottle, put my feet up, and tried to think out the implications of everything.

Was I really going to endorse the spiels that "Aelita" and "Tinidril" had tried to sell me in my dreams? The call to action, to be some kind of Chosen One who would save the world? Was I going to become a warrior in the battle to save the timeline from invasion from the future? Or was I just going to focus on my current assignment, trying to find Holger Holtzclaw, and maybe get into Juniper Holtzclaw's pants? And who was issuing my marching orders? LUCA? Was LUCA identical to AEOTA? Was DUCA the Dark Archon?

Several shots later, nothing seemed any clearer to me, and I had drawn no solid conclusions, nor made any solid plans.

My Nokia rang. It was Marty Quartz, my ebullient tech guy.

"Vern, how's it hanging? Listen, you got me interested in this aeota business. I noodled around on the web some more and found something interesting. Why don't you come over and see what I turned up? It should be quick, because Burning Man's just around the corner."

"Sure. Tomorrow around noon okay?"

"You bet. I'm busy today anyhow. LARPing."

"Lopping?"

"No, man. *LARPing*. Live-action role playing. Me and the crew are doing a few hours of Joyce's *Ulysses*. It's mostly an excuse to wear tweed and bar-hop and get drunk and talk about sex."

"Okay then. Have an extra stout for me." I thanked Marty in advance for his help tomorrow, cut off the call and got up to leave. The tequila had had as much effect on my shattered brain as if it had been so much water.

57

The Nokia signaled another call, this time from Yulia. I hoped she wasn't still freaking out about that absurd ransom note.

Her voice was uncommonly, frighteningly affectionate. She sounded almost like the early days of our marriage.

"Hi, Vern. How's your day going?"

"Um—okay, I guess."

"I'm glad. Listen, on your way home, could you grab something for supper. Nothing hard to cook, maybe hot dogs or a pound of hamburger. Hell, maybe you'd better just make it sushi or a frozen pizza. And don't forget—you promised to buy Aelita the new issue of that comic she likes."

12 Homecoming

My involuntary-bachelor digs consisted of a studio apartment at the Palmer Old Ditch Arms, a rundown barf-colored stucco complex, built around the time Norma Jeane Mortenson was first contemplating changing her name, hard by the festering former nineteenth-century canal that loaned its moniker to the place, in a neighborhood where stripped bicycle carcasses chained to telephone poles were deemed elegant street furniture.

When I got to the place after fumfumming an answer and hanging up on Yulia, I stopped at the front door. The nameplate next to my accustomed bell-push read JACK BOLAN. I took out my key ring, and discovered that the key to the outer door was missing, along with the inner one.

The place boasted no super, so I rang the bell for the apartment next to mine. Never a guy famous for neighborliness, I knew that resident by sight anyhow, if not by name: an elderly retired Jewish guy who seldom left his rooms.

I saw his heel-trodden slippers first, coming down the staircase visible through the dirty beveled glass of the front door. Then the rest of his inglorious figure came into view, all warts and gristle, watery eyes and a combover, animating a food-stained bathrobe.

He did not move to unlock the door. "Yes? What do you want? If you are selling the usual *dreck und kipple*, you should *gai feifen ahfen yam*, why don't you, please?"

I didn't even bother to respond. It was plain as the bribes sticking out of a politician's pocket that Mr. Neighbor Man had never seen me before.

Back in my car, I drove slowly away, trying to rationalize this turn of events.

My tenure in the Archean era and on Venus had somehow sent me back to a changed world. An entirely different continuum to my point of origin? Or my unique natal timeline somehow reconfigured? In the first case, I might hold out hopes for returning to the *status quo ante* by somehow slipping sidewise across the multiverse. But in the second scenario, all bets were off. And either alternative presented me with no easy visible exit.

So I figured I had to make the best of things for the time being, until something new developed.

So I was still married to Yulia. And with a daughter to boot. Who'da thunk it? It took me a while to wrap my mind around the notion. After a while, it didn't seem like such a horrible fate. So long as my Ukrainian hellcat had not yet learned her argument-winning tactic of smashing one of the Trypillya ceramic animal figurines from her collection atop my noggin. Not that she had ever done so without justifiable provocation.

My first stop was a liquor store for a bottle of Yulia's favorite Ukrainian bison grass vodka. A lot pricier than Old Sandstone, but sure to be received happily.

Next I hit up a supermarket on the edge of the city as I headed toward the old doublewide. (I had just assumed Yulia and Aelita and I were still living in the trailer park. But a sudden worry jumped up at me: What if, in this world, we weren't? Awfully awkward to call home and ask for the address.) I ravaged the prepared-food steam tables like Cortez looking for silver tchotchkes, and soon had a dozen Styrofoam clamshells filled with edible goodies. I added some orange juice for the vodka and some soda for the kid, and felt golden.

Back on the highway, I suddenly remembered Yulia's closing injunction: "And don't forget—you promised to buy Aelita the new issue of that comic she likes."

What the hell would that be? And where did one find comics in this day and age? Conditions had changed, I knew, since I was a kid, when every drugstore carried them.

A few miles from home, conveniently on the same side of the road, I spotted the sign for MIDICHLORIAN COMICS. Whether the place was newly established with the birth of this alternate universe, or had always been present even in my old timeline, I couldn't say. Who has every evanescent shop along their commute memorized?

The windowless door bore the legend "The right to buy comics is the right to be free." To announce my entry, the door emitted a raygun noise as I opened it. No other customers were about.

From the back emerged a trim young woman, kinda goth-nerd with pink-streaked hair. Her outfit featured more buckles and leather straps than those of all Four Musketeers combined. I had been expecting a fat middle-aged guy, so I uncomfortably hemmed and hawed for a minute with my question. I was also disconcerted by not knowing exactly how old my own daughter was. She couldn't be more than five, so I settled for that.

Trying to sound for the first time ever like a real Concerned Dad, I asked, "What kind of comics do you have that are suitable for a little girl in the first grade or thereabouts?"

Disconcertingly, the woman smelled like fresh-cut grass. "Well, there's a lot of franchise characters, Scooby-Doo and such. But I really like this indie one by Pris Cohen."

From a rack she reached down an issue of *Aeota*. The colorful cover depicted a pastoral scene full of whimsical monsters and one Alice / Pollyanna / Anne of Green Gables / Pippi Longstocking avatar.

"What this creator has done is really unique. She's taken an antique character from a forgotten newspaper strip, a weird little girl herself, and brought her into the twenty-first century. Made her modern without losing the nostalgic charm."

A memory of my online research from—was it possible?—just earlier today returned to me. "You're talking about Herbert Crowley's *The Wigglemuch*."

The woman's eyes lit up. The tip of her tongue popped out innocently to wet just one corner of her lips, and she stepped closer to me. If I hadn't been heading home to Yulia, I knew I could have been heading home with her.

"You know the Wigglemuch! Cool beans!"

"I get around. Is this the newest issue?"

"Just out this week."

"I'll take it. Oh, do you have any back issues too?"

"Sure, the whole run. The book's only up to number five."

"Toss 'em in."

I left the store with blue balls that ached too much for someone who had just been banging a hot Venusian broad only a couple of hours ago.

The trailer park where I had ensconced my brood upon the fortuitous acquisition of our Fleetwood Homes Hopewell model doublewide—two beds, one bath, eight-hundred-and-forty square feet, on sale for $35K!—was named Owl in Daylight Courts and featured on its signboard an image of a rather stunned-looking bird. I drove through the estate to our tiny lot. The Hopewell looked impossibly improved from when I had visited Yulia just a few subjective hours ago: flowers around the temporary foundation, curtains in the windows, a kid's tricycle near the steps.

I got out of the car, climbed the stairs, turned the unlocked doorknob, pushed inward, and called out, "Honey, I'm home!"

13 BEDTIME STORY

WHEN I SAW YULIA STANDING JUST INSIDE THE trailer, I remembered why I had originally fallen in love with her. Her thick dark hair, plaited and pinned up, gleamed. Her self-assured posture spoke somehow of a strong indifference to any unfair blows, such as exile from her native land, that fate might have dealt or yet have in store. The genetically forced yet subtle show of her two front teeth framed by those "incompetent lips" was very sexy. And her figure was aces too.

When she smiled widely at my arrival, instead of frowning and hurling fishwife abuse at me, I felt a sharp pang of guilt and regret that I had ever helped in any way to sour and undo our first affections, thanks to my tomcatting and general lackluster vocational efforts and reluctance to procreate.

I had no idea where this whole Aeota affair was leading, whether I was embarked on a mission to save the universe, or merely falling down a rabbit hole of insanity; whether I would follow up on all of the things that had happened to me in just one day, or completely ignore them. But whatever eventuated, I sensed and believed that this reunion or renewal—if you could apply such terms to a state of affairs that had paradoxically never ended in the first place on this timeline—was something good and desirable.

I set my groceries down on the dining room table—a beat-up piece from the local salvage merchandise depot—and embraced Yulia like a drowning sailor clutching a handy dolphin. She seemed surprised for a moment, but then reciprocated just as heartily. The slight accent to her next words only added to her charms.

"Hey, rough customer, don't crumple the merchandise!"

Yulia's grasp of idioms had never matched her intelligence nor facility with standard syntax.

I released her and stepped back. "Guess I just missed you, kiddo."

"You've only been gone since ten this morning."

"Yeah, well, it felt like half a billion years."

Yulia turned and began unpacking the containers of food. Three place settings—paper plates, paper napkins, plastic utensils—already suggested a warm family dinnertime. Two spots featured wine glasses, and the third hosted a worn plastic tumbler from Mickey D's featuring an all-but-obliterated Lilo & Stitch.

"You went wild, Vern. There's enough here for three meals!"

"I haven't eaten in a very long time."

"You should never shop when you're hungry. My mother told me that."

Yulia had arranged the containers on the tabletop to her esthetic and practical satisfaction. I mixed two vodka-and-OJs. "Lita! Your daddy's home and it's time to eat!"

Out from one of the two bedrooms scampered a miniature Yulia, dressed in a green fleece top and pants. This was not the exact child I had met in the Archean, but scarily close enough. I thought to see some of my legacy in her stocky build. But thankfully she was all Yulia elsewhere, right down to the dentally indiscreet lips. Kid would break hearts someday.

Halfway to me, she screamed, "Catch me, Daddy!" and hurled herself impossibly through the air as if launched from an invisible diving board. I reacted pretty well, almost as if I had done this kind of thing before.

In my arms, half-smothering me with her squirmy embrace, which smelled of child musk, spilled apple juice, and Play-Doh, Aelita planted a bevy of kisses atop my head. Eventually I managed to unwrap her anaconda coils and set her down.

"Did you bring me a comic, Daddy?"

I had folded the several comics in half lengthwise and stuck the whole bag in a back pocket of my pants. "Yeah, sure, here they are."

"*Dad*-dy! You folded them! Now they're not in mint condition!"

"Lita! Tell your father thank you!"

"Oh, right! Thanks, Daddy. You couldn't help that you just didn't know any better."

"Agreed." My daughter's criticism didn't seem bratty to me or overwrought, but rather charming. Maybe I was just a sucker for anyone who lavished kisses on my poor benighted head.

Aelita took the comics out of the bag. "Why'd you buy these old ones? We have them already."

"Guess I forgot."

She shuffled the new one out of the pack and studied the cover intently.

"You know the rules, Lita. No reading at the table."

Obediently she set the comic aside and climbed into her chair. She stared hungrily at the array of food, and I wondered what she would pick first. I hoped I wouldn't be asked to dole out her favorite food.

Yulia had clasped her hands together prayerfully. This had not been a feature of our childless mealtimes back in the old contentious universe. But I guessed having a kid had reactivated Yulia's own childhood religious customs.

"The hungry shall eat and be satisfied and those who seek the Lord shall praise Him, their hearts shall live forever. Amen."

Aelita and I both chimed in on the "Amen." Then Lita said, "Pass me the sushi, please."

Okay. I had a sophisticated kid. The apple does not fall far from the tree.

Yulia savored her cocktail, which I had made pretty strong. Lita got apple juice. Then we all swarmed to eating like Napoleon's troops in retreat from Russia falling upon a peasant's well-stocked larder.

When we were finished I said, "You guys sit, I'll do the cleanup."

"Oh, sure, on the night we use paper plates."

"There's still three glasses to wash. That's gotta earn me some points."

I went into the kitchen and found a reasonably familiar setting in which I felt at ease. I cleaned the glasses, then impulsively looked in the freezer.

"Hey, there's ice cream!"

"Yay!" came Aelita's seconding of my implicit proposal.

We all enjoyed a Polar Bar apiece. Aelita's face ended up smeared with chocolate. Then Yulia said, "Just enough time for your bath and bedtime reading, girl."

Aelita's solemn expression charmed the socks off me. I could get used to this domestic scene.

"I know, Mama."

Yulia shepherded our daughter into the bathroom. At the door, she stopped to look back at me.

"I've got plans later for you, rough customer."

I kicked idly around the doublewide, feeling at once foreign and utterly at home, floating a bit from the booze and the crazy day, while Aelita succumbed to being scrubbed. She emerged in pajamas decorated with those little green gremlins from, I think, *Toy Story*.

"Okay," said Yulia to me. "Your turn to parent."

Having seen Aelita come out of her own bedroom, I did not hesitate, but steered her right to bed. I noticed that the walls of her room were covered with her own very competent drawings. She had snagged the new issue of *Aeota* on the way and, once snuggled under the covers, handed it to me. I sat in an adjacent folding chair with a ripped padded seat, and began to read aloud the comic's word balloons. The Aeota character, confronting a gnarly, involuted old man, spoke first.

"Oh, hello, Mister After All. What are you doing here?"

"No, Daddy! Use the Aeota voice!"

I tried to remember what the abnormal little girl had sounded like half a billion years ago, and repeated the lines.

"Perfect!"

We only got halfway through the story—a surreal farrago about an invasion of Aeota's idyllic native countryside, full of quirky non-human characters—when Aelita fell asleep. I shut off the light and exited quietly, closing her door behind me.

I went to the bathroom, which was all steamy from someone's recent perfumed shower. I used the toilet and the shower myself, then found the master bedroom.

Yulia was waiting naked for me. My dick got stiff as the limb of a petrified pine tree. She hurled herself at me in the manner of her daughter, but with no innocent intent.

68

We banged away for a satisfying interval, and then when I orgasmed, the world disappeared again, as it had done when I was screwing the Green Lady.

This could become a bad habit, and definitely ruin a guy's sex life.

14 INTERVIEW WITH A DESCENDANT

THE SUN ALOFT WAS, AGAIN, LESS INTENSE THAN what I was used to in my everyday existence. But unlike the orb that lit the Archean, this luminary did not portray the immaturity of youth, suggestive of a more forceful and vibrant, happy heyday ahead. This was, rather, a senile sun, reddish-orange like a tangerine, slowly guttering out to a final extinction, begrudging every photon it had to share with its ungrateful planetary children.

Disoriented as I was from the insane transition, I could still recognize that this phenomenon was all screwy, counterfactual. I knew the sun was only supposed to get hotter for the next few hundred million years. Its expansive end stages as a red giant would have meant the evaporation of the Earth. This impossible weak but stable condition was straight out of some old Superman comic or sci-fi fantasy.

Or maybe someone had tampered with our star over the eons?

Underneath my naked back was the familiar undulant vegetable mat, stretching as far as I could see when I tentatively sat up. But unlike the similar raft in the Archean, this gray-brown mat seemed salty and sticky and slightly putrescent, a sickly thing.

I stood up, and when I did, I could see some kind of far-off structure, gleaming white. I began walking toward it, employing a sailor's rolling gait to accommodate the mild waves.

Hours seemed to pass. I got pretty thirsty, but didn't care to sample the waters below the mat, suspecting them of being undrinkably foul. My sensations of thirst were remarkably painful and intense for a hallucination. And it had to be a hallucination, didn't it?

At the end of an interminable interval, my destination became recognizable. After a fashion.

The structure was the horned skull of some non-human creature, and it was as big as Michigan Stadium. A hundred thousand souls could have taken up residence inside, if they had been content with single-room occupancy. The shape of the skull suggested a cross between a dragon, a platypus, and a panda—a thing that only millions of years of evolution under strange conditions could have spawned. Much too massive to be floating, it must be resting atop solid land, some weathered nub of Amasia or Novopangaea, the future continents.

The fossil had no lower jaw, which must have come unhinged and gotten lost during its posthumous travels. But giant fangs projecting from the upper jaw and functioning as pillars served to keep the mouth entrance accessible, as if I were walking under some bone canopy into an exclusive nightclub.

Inside the skull, light penetrated through eye sockets, ear holes, and some cranial gaps. There was nothing artificial inside, just the ivory acreage.

"Hello! Tinidril? Aelita? Anyone home?"

Those were the only two beings I could imagine inhabiting this place, my ancestral and Venusian girlfriends.

My eye was attracted by a motion far, far up near the skull's ceiling. A figure was descending, dropping down leisurely through the stuffy air with no visible means of support. At first a mere dot, it naturally assumed more definition the closer it got. When it was about thirty feet high, I recognized who it was.

Mister After All, the crippled and contorted oldster from the *Aeota* comic I had just been reading to my daughter. Dressed in a raggedy black fustian suit, he sported a goatlike chin beard, axe-blade nose, rheumy eyes, and wild white tufts of hair on either side of a bald liver-spotted dome.

He touched down lightly on the floor and leered up at me from his twisted scoliosis stance, like a crippled flamingo with its neck in a knot. His voice creaked like a desiccated wooden signboard swinging on rusty hooks in an arid desert ghost town.

"Welcome to what must be, and what must backwards forever become."

"You're DUCA. The uh, the uh—"

"Descendant Ultimately Converged from All. But of course."

"Why did you bring me here?"

"I am seeking your cooperation. Your resistance will avail you naught in the end. I will have my way. But your cooperation will help me in some small measure. So of course, like any rational being, I prefer it."

"You expect me to help you extend this wasteland back in time to meet LUCA?"

"Precisely. I need to merge with my bride. I yearn for her. She calls to me."

"You might yearn, pal, but I don't hear her calling. And what's in it for me if I help? If you change the past to be all-slime-all-the-time, where does that leave me?"

"You will continue to have a very satisfying virtual existence within me, along with all the rest of your kind who have ever existed down the ages. But I will grant a greater agency within the emulation to those who help me. You will be like a god, able to use others as your playthings."

"Forget it! I'm not gonna sell out every human who ever lived."

Mister After All smacked his lips and tut-tutted gently. "Oh, well, that's too bad. But if I can't get your allegiance, then I won't brook your interference. Prepare to die."

His words, delivered evenly and without bravado or belligerence, were more frightening for their equanimity and assurance than any ranting threat could have been. I took a step backwards, then another—then turned and ran.

I made it outside before he caught up to me with improbable speed, his bent legs scissoring like clockwork. In all likelihood he had been merely letting me feel an instant of false, futile freedom before he snatched it effortlessly away. He leaped upon me—the third person to do so in such a short time—and before I quite realized what was happening, we were rising through the air.

"I shall drop you to shatter upon these ancient bones like a gull drops a clam upon a rock."

I squirmed and fought, but to no purpose.

We were scores of feet above the skull when Mister After All came to a stop in midair.

"Good riddance, human."

Released, I plummeted.

I was proud I didn't scream. But I did shut my eyes tight as a bank vault.

The next sensation I felt was not a bone-splintering thud but a huge wet embrace. I opened my eyes.

An enormous vegetable tendril had erupted from the ocean mat. Green and healthy looking, its anomalous bulk moved with some intelligence and direction.

Mister After All screeched like a raptor and arrowed toward us.

The tendril morphed to englobe me protectively, as the mat had done back in the Vaalbara room. The sphere filled with a pungent smell, and I passed out.

15 Double, Double, Out of the Bubble

Waking, I instantly felt a deep déjà vu. Somehow, I knew, I had done all this before.

I opened my eyes and realized the literal truth of my sensations.

Once more I was recumbent upon the sandy cement floor of the empty Vaalbara room at AEOTA HQ, wearing the same clothes I had had on since breakfast, a meal that seemed millennia ago. Sunlight poured through the gashes in the roof.

Starting miles away around midnight, my orgasm-induced astral travel had brought me to the Dying Earth to confront DUCA, and then back to this locale during daylight hours, courtesy of my tentacled rescuer, Aeota or Aelita or LUCA or the Green Lady. But what amount of time had passed? When was I? A sudden pang struck me. Could I have already lost my new life with Yulia and Aelita, after just a few hours of domestic pleasure, from being cast forward in time, in effect abandoning them with seeming heartlessness and offering no notice or explanation?

I jumped up and raced to the ladder on the wall.

Recently dislodged flakes of rust seemed to show it had just been used.

I clambered up onto the platform, then rushed through the airlock into the suiting-up chamber.

The locker where I had found my possessions in an old liquor box was empty, and the liquor box itself rested on the floor where I had once discarded it.

I dashed through the rest of the deserted building and emerged outside just in time to see my car drive off.

Naturally, the other me was behind the wheel, oblivious to anyone, even his doppelganger, shouting and jumping and gesticulating in the rearview mirror.

I slumped, then turned to look at the building's façade.

The crumbling signage atop the place did not announce a candy company. Instead, it read:

AEOTA MOTORS

GREEN MACHINES FOR A GREEN FUTURE

Did the changed sign mean that I had slipped tracks again in the multiverse? If so, would the differences be significant or trivial?

I wouldn't find any answers standing here, so I started to walk.

Out on the main highway, such as it was, I expected to smell the forest fires that had accompanied my drive here. Maybe even see some distant smoke. But nada. The country air was clean as a church lavatory.

I tried to recall if the Vern Ruggles in the car had encountered any different environmental conditions on the drive back during my earlier retreat from the ruined HQ. But no memories came to me. I figured I had been too intent on getting home then to notice.

Now that I had attained the two-lane road, I tried to hitch a ride. But traffic was infrequent, and after a while I just gave up, figuring

I'd focus on finding a phone and arranging for some old-fashioned transport. First house or business I saw, I'd make a call on a borrowed phone. Even if I had had my Nokia, I would've had to go old school; it didn't support the Uber app.

Although the strange way the device had been acting lately, who knew what magic pumpkin-and-mice coach it might have summoned for me?

I was walking in the same direction as the adjacent traffic was flowing, so I did not see the antique yet immaculate ranger-green pickup truck until it passed me and pulled over to the shoulder not far ahead. Its storage bed was piled high with securely strapped wooden crates.

The driver's door opened and a bearded man got out. I felt like I should know him somehow.

About ten feet away, I flashed on his identity.

He was the young white hipster from the Aeota Farm, who had explained the barnside tobacco advertisement to me and given me a dozen eggs. (Had those eggs still been in my car when I drove off a few minutes ago? Another thing I could not remember, due to my distraction at the time.) Sure enough, the truck's door bore the farm's name and crest, and inside the cab sat his partner, the round-faced young black woman with the fountain of frizzy hair.

"Hey man, you need a ride?"

"Yes! Yes, I do! Where are you going?"

"Into the city to make a delivery."

"Perfect! You can't imagine how grateful I am."

"Slide in then."

I went to the passenger door. The woman had already scooted her butt over to the middle of the bench seat.

We were on the road again in just a few seconds.

"I'm Vern Ruggles."

"You didn't tell us your name a few hours ago when we chatted," said the woman.

Okay, so there was some useful continuity.

"I'm Philip Kendrick Langham. And this is Martha Washington."

The woman's name activated another college-age literary memory, about the same vintage as my *Perelandra* reading experience, pertaining to a certain graphic novel.

"Who's the president of the USA?" I asked.

The woman scowled. "Erwin Rexall."

My face must have looked as if I had stumbled onto a dozen bloody corpses. I could feel a cold sweat break out across my brow.

The man and woman both laughed uproariously.

"Just messing with you," Martha said. "My folks named me after the Frank Miller story, and I can't resist seeing if anyone picks up on it."

"So the president isn't Erwin Rexall."

"Nah, it's still *him*."

"That's the only time I have ever been grateful to hear that."

"What happened to your car?" Langham said.

"A close friend needed it more than I did."

"Well, that's pretty generous of you."

"You'd do the same in my shoes, I'm sure."

The rest of the ride into the city was passed with general pleasantries. Langham and Washington were good people, if a tad naive.

"I really think the future will be better than the present," Washington said at one point, earning a sage nod from Langham.

"Well, I myself am definitely working toward such a goal," I said.

Back in the city, I could not reasonably ask my saviors to detour from their deadline-determined delivery route—a series of restaurants and organic grocery co-ops—and so by the time they dropped me off at my office and we said our pleasant farewells, it was much later than my avatar's visit there.

I secured my spare office key from its hiding place under a large flowerpot next to the rickety elevator on my level. Inside, my counterpart had considerately left some tequila for me and I drained the bottle. I dug out some cash from my safe—not that my reserves were sizable—and called for a conventional cab.

I had plenty of time to think, on the way to the Palmer Old Ditch Trailer Park. But I conceived of no surefire plan of action.

Passing MIDICHLORIAN COMICS, I had a whimsical impulse to stop in, hoping maybe for a quickie with the clerk. But the place was dark and shuttered for the night.

I had the cabbie drop me off at the low-rent estate's entrance. Darkness had descended. I worked my way circuitously around to Yulia's doublewide, trying not to look like a peeping tom or cat burglar. Maybe any fellow residents who spotted me would recognize me as a neighbor and assume I was just out for a stroll. Although what they would think if they had seen me enter Yulia's home but not exit by any conventional means was another matter.

Eventually I hunkered down behind a bridal veil shrub not far from the trailer. I heard laughter and voices from inside but couldn't make out any words. That was okay. The whole night was still fresh in my memory.

It got to be roughly the hour when Aelita had fallen asleep. Any time now I'd start having sex with Yulia, then presumably vanish into the future that hosted DUCA. I had some half-assed plan in mind to rush back in when she started screaming at my sudden disappearance and pretend I had leaped up and fallen out a window or something. But for that story to make any sense at all, wouldn't I have to be naked? Should I start stripping now?

As things happened, the necessity to act was removed from me.

I heard my own copulatory grunting and groans reach a crescendo inside the trailer. ("If this timeline is rocking, don't come knocking.") Then, at the moment of my climax I felt what I could only term a kind of doubling of my consciousness, a fleeting overlay of two identities, past and present, Vern and Vern +1, as my existential loop closed.

And then I was back in bed, naked atop Yulia, filling the cosmic niche my earlier self had just involuntarily vacated.

Yulia grabbed my ears and pulled my face down for a kiss.

"Was that good for you, honey?"

"It was a trip, baby—a real trip."

16 TAKE YOUR DAUGHTER TO WORK DAY

WHEN I WOKE UP THE NEXT MORNING, FOR THE
first few seconds I expected to discover myself lying on the factory floor again, a forgotten remnant of the whole dicey AEOTA
enterprise, whether affinity-totalizing, candy-making, or auto-man-
ufacturing, just another piece of debris. That forlorn place seemed
to be my go-to crash pad lately. But, happily, I wasn't there. Instead,
I was stretched out in a pleasantly rumpled, woman-smelling con-
jugal bed inside the doublewide.

Yulia was not beside me, but I did not worry, because I could
hear productive, mundane, bustling-around-type noises beyond the
closed door.

I had never had a night's sleep like the one that had just passed. It
had been more like anesthesia than sleep. I could not recall a single
dream, twitch, urge to piss, impulse to roll over, proximity of a bed
partner, or ache of a sore hip. I guessed that was my reward for
staying awake for a few billion years, and hopscotching across space
and time. Whatever the cause, I felt invigorated and renewed. I was
ready to tackle this whole crazy mystery that had been dropped in
my lap. I had a real sense that today I would make some progress.

Although why I should have felt so sanguine, what with the lousy cards I was holding, I had no idea.

My leads to any kind of conspiratorial corporate AEOTA had vanished, due to the impossibly ancient abandonment of their building upstate. I didn't see any way of confirming or using the uncanny material I had learned from LUCA or DUCA or the Green Lady—assuming all that wasn't pure hallucination. Not promising.

But I still had Juniper Holtzclaw to question some more. After all, the disappearance of her husband had arguably triggered all this, and he had been confirmed as a visitor to the office of Thomas T. Thaumas & Co. And Marty Quartz had uncovered something new. I was to see him today at noon.

The memory made me jump up and fumble for my Nokia in my pile of discarded clothes. (I had dropped them in a heap when I first entered the bedroom last night after showering.) The phone told me it was only eight-thirty, so I could relax. And it had no additional enigmatic texts to trouble me.

The bedroom closet and bureau held lots of my familiar clothes. Naturally enough. I lived here, right, pater familias? I assembled a new clean outfit—a green-striped Oxford shirt and khaki pants—then transferred all the contents of my old pockets to the new pants. That included the two strips of paper printed out by the Nokia and the charm bracelet that had been delivered to my office.

In doing so, I noticed that the bracelet had been changed somehow to conform to the second text message. Three of the charms remained the same, but instead of a magnifying glass there dangled a little explosion icon.

All decked out, I made a quick trip to the toilet, had a swift shave, and then ambled out to the dining nook.

Yulia and Aelita, dressed for the day, were waiting on breakfast for me. Platters of pancakes and bacon. Smelled like heaven. Yulia was beaming with a concupiscent afterglow that was almost mortifying to me. Aelita busily perused her comic book, but had the grace and affection and manners to put it aside when I arrived.

"Good morning, Daddy. Happy Saturday!"

"How did you sleep, Vern?"

"Like the proverbial King Arthur van Winkle." I kissed Yulia on the lips and Aelita on the brow, then slid into my seat. "Send those flapjacks and rashers my way."

Aelita giggled. "Flapjacks!"

Yulia said, "We almost didn't have them, since we were out of eggs. But I found a dozen out in your car, Vern, when I went to fill the tank. I figured you'd probably be running on fumes, and it might help you. You really should have brought them inside last night. But they still seemed okay—and they all had double yolks!"

I recalled getting the eggs from the Aeota Farm folks. Was it okay to eat them? I was too famished to worry.

After I had inhaled about a half-pound of bacon and six or ten pancakes, as well as a quart of coffee, I pushed back from the table contentedly.

"What's your schedule like today, Vern?"

"I've got to work for at least a few hours. Is that okay?"

"Is it still that Holtzclaw job?"

Yulia's question was reassuring in its evident link to the timeline I had come from. "Yeah. I need to visit the grieving wife again. I think she's holding out on some important facts."

"Do you think you could take Lita with you? It's safe enough, isn't it? Nothing bad she shouldn't hear or see?"

The request took me aback. But as I thought it over, I figured, why not?

"Yeah, she can come. I'll just stash her in another room if I think I have to dredge up anything nasty with Juniper. But I also have to see Marty at noon."

Aelita chimed in. "I like Mister Quartz. He reminds me of the Genie."

"What Genie?"

"From *Aladdin*, Daddy! How could you forget? We've seen it like a million million times!"

I tried to imagine sitting in front of the TV with this child, playing the same DVD over and over from night to night. What had happened to my avatar who had lived out all those domestic hours? Had my entrance to his world displaced him, canceled him out? Had we somehow merged, as I had merged last night with my earlier pre-orgasmic self? If so, why hadn't I acquired his unique memories? Why had I remained a stranger to this new set of circumstances? No obvious answers came to me.

"Oh, right, of course," I said. "Good old Robin Williams."

Yulia looked puzzled. "Robin Williams? Wasn't that Sam Kinison? I think Williams died way before *Aladdin*."

"What was I thinking? Sure, Kinison was the Genie."

Yulia's look brightened. "Well, if you can take Lita, I'd appreciate it. I'm supposed to be volunteering at the hospital front desk today."

"Don't give it a second thought. Lita and I together will outdo Watson and Holmes."

"Who?"

I shut up before I said anything else that was dangerously counterfactual and might land me in the bughouse.

17 RIDE WITH A WELL-KNOWN STRANGER

OUTSIDE OUR TRAILER IN THE GRAVEL PARKING
area, Yulia marched to her car: a beater equally as vintage as mine,
which I recognized from our prior divorced life. Except that its
familiar blue rusted chassis now sported the hood badge of AEOTA
MOTORS, a kind of postmodern triskelion of fractal complexity.
This model was apparently a "Viridian."

Leaning into the back of her car, Yulia extracted a child's booster
seat.

"Here, you'll need this."

"Mommy, Mommy, can I ride in the front with Daddy? Please,
please, please?"

"You really shouldn't . . . "

"Aw, c'mon, Yule—does Robin ride behind Batman in the Batmo-
bile, or alongside?"

"Robin? Robin's worked for the Joker for twenty years now."

I slapped my forehead in exaggerated fashion, lolled out my
tongue, and made the face of a dumb yokel, eliciting some more
giggles from Aelita. "Guess I'd better stop in at Midichlorian Comics
more often."

Yulia frowned. "Not because of that trampy Goth clerk, I hope!"

"Yulia, baby! I am no longer that same old Vern Ruggles you once knew."

And truer words were never spoken.

After some more perfunctory tsk-tsking, Yulia consented to the minor safety violation and fastened the booster device in place in the shotgun seat of my car. Thank God, because I had no idea how to do it.

"You'd better drive extra safe."

"Like I'm carrying the whole world in that seat."

I belted in Aelita, kissed Yulia goodbye while grabbing her ass for reassuring good measure, then got behind the wheel. Motoring off, I saw my newly restored wife waving to us in the rearview mirror, a wistful smile on her face at the thought of all this daddy-daughter bonding.

Once on the highway, I cast a brief sidewise glance at my daughter. She was observing the passing scenery with all the deliberative gravitas of Jehovah contemplating His handiwork on the day after creation. I couldn't begin to fathom her thoughts.

Something was pinching one of my thighs. It was the angular charm bracelet in my right front pants pocket, made irksome by the leg motions of driving. I pulled over to the breakdown lane, put the car in PARK and dug out the geegaw. For some reason, I recalled that the carnies used to call this kind of cheap jewelry "slum."

"Lita? Would you like to wear this?"

The kid didn't reply, but simply regarded me soberly and held out her left arm.

I undid the clasp and draped the four tokens on their thin chain around her little wrist. I hadn't really registered the size of the bracelet before now, whether it was meant for an adult or for a child, but suddenly it seemed to writhe and shrink itself to fit the child's dimensions perfectly. I secured the clasp with an audible click.

I looked up from Aelita's wrist, and it wasn't her any longer.

Strapped into the booster seat, inhabiting Aelita's outfit of jelly sandals, pink stretch pants, and a white T-shirt decorated with a finned blue dinosaur-type Pokémon labeled "Dialga," was the preternatural child of the Archean Age with whom I had strolled naked across the world-girdling microbial mat, her features a curious caricature or morphosis of the mortal Aelita's.

The kid's voice was mature and assured. "Thank you for bringing me into this particular present, Vern. Now I can help you."

"No. Stop this. Go away and give me my daughter back."

"But I am your daughter, Vern. Just as much as I am the mother of everyone."

"Are you LUCA?"

"I am. But I am also—" And again she uttered that curiously stereophonic name that sounded like "Aelita" and "Aeota" conjoined.

"Listen, I know you only mean well. But I can't afford to get mixed up in this. I'm living in a world now that seems pretty swell. I've got a wife and a daughter, and I'm not sitting alone on a Saturday night sucking booze from a jam jar in a dirty bathrobe. You're going to have to solve this beef with DUCA or the Dark Archon or whoever it is that you're fighting with on your own, without my help."

"You won't have a daughter or wife if you don't help me, Vern. They will all be taken away from you. And everyone else in all the worlds throughout all the many timelines will lose their loved ones as well."

"Bullshit! I can't be the linchpin of this whole insane crusade."

"But you are. Just as many others also are. Each of you unique and invaluable and essential."

I reached down for Lita's wrist. She allowed me to grip it without resistance. I tried to undo the clasp on the bracelet, but it wouldn't give.

"You see, Vern. This is how things must be."

I rested my head on the steering wheel. The low thrumming of the car's idling engine seemed to expand and resonate until it filled the whole universe with a celestial purr. I found the white noise reassuring somehow, as if I had tapped into the remnant background hum of the ancient Big Bang.

I raised my face up from the wheel, no doubt with its knurled pattern embossed on my brow.

"All right. Where do we go from here?"

"Just where you were planning to go. To the Holtzclaw house. We have to rescue Holger Holtzclaw. He's got something for us."

18 HOLTZCLAW IN HELL

JUNIPER HOLTZCLAW'S CAR OCCUPIED ITS USUAL
spot in her long impressive driveway, so I assumed she was home.
She didn't go out much anyhow, fearing recognition in public due
to her husband's infamy. And almost all her former *bon ton* friends
had disowned her.

As we walked across the drive from where I had parked, I experienced a nearly overwhelming sense of chronal displacement, a
kind of simultaneous attenuation and enlargement of each passing
second, related to my last visit here, which seemed both irretrievably removed and also just accomplished. I halted and began to
sway. Then I felt Aelita's small warm hand slither into mine—the
same touch that had once sent me to Perelandra.

But this time her touch was stabilizing. Just as suddenly as it had
come, the dizzy wave of temporal deracination left me, and I was
able to walk on.

Standing on the stoop after ringing the bell, I glanced down at her
suspiciously.

Her voice had reverted to normal childlike tones and diction,
but she still looked waveringly off-model, like my daughter pulled

Alice-style through a funhouse mirror. One invariant factor was those damnably cute incompetent lips.

"Daddy, are we still going to see Mister Quartz next?"

"Yes, we are. That is, if you don't do something screwy here and mess things up."

"What do you mean, Daddy?"

"You know goddamn well what I mean."

"Don't swear, Daddy. You know Mommy doesn't like it."

The door opened cautiously. A slice of Holtzclaw physiognomy revealed itself. Then the door swung wider.

"Come in. Hurry!"

Juniper Holtzclaw still looked mostly like the winning ticket in a multi-state lottery whose pot nobody had broken in several months of doubling. Today she wore a one-piece playsuit of a type I had seen a lot of this season. The fabric was a kind of lace-work, like a cro-cheted doily, only sexy, over a silky underlayer. Cut high on the legs and low on the bust, the outfit seemed to say, "I can't decide whether to play croquet or ball your brains out."

But her killer appearance was diminished by an expensive hairdo disheveled as if by constant plowing with nervous fingers, and a haggard face. Raccoon eyes, red nose.

"Thank God you're here," she said, gripping me by one wrist. "You've got to do something to help me. You've got to find Holger, so he stops sending me these bad dreams! I can't get any rest!"

"Nightmares? What are they like?"

She released me and raked her hair. "They're always the same. Holger is trapped in some kind of prison cell made out of horrid decaying slimy materials, like rotten seaweed or something. He's begging me to help him get free. And then someone—some creature like an ancient geezer—comes and starts to torture him gruesomely! That's when I wake up screaming."

Juniper collapsed against me and began to sob. I patted her back in a fashion as friendly as my irresponsibly swelling penis would allow.

Aelita tugged on my shirt and whispered just loud enough for me to hear her above Juniper's crying. "DUCA has him. When he visited Thaumas, they took him. You've got to go rescue him. He has a thing we need."

Juniper straightened up and took cognizance of Aelita for the first time. "Who's this? Your daughter? Why is she here?"

"I can't find anyone to mind her. She drove her last babysitter straight to Bellevue. Poor woman was convinced she had been sent on a trip to Venus. I hate to say it, but this one's a bad seed. I think I'd better stow her in the car. You just wait here a minute."

I brought Aelita outside.

"How the hell am I going to jump across four billion years to find Holtzclaw? And if I can get there, how do I rescue him?"

"You know how to time travel. Just like you did before, when you had sex with Yulia. You have to have sex with this woman now. And when you get to the future, there'll be help."

Despite the knowledge that I was speaking to a four-billion-year-old entity, I was shocked to hear this extramarital injunction coming from the mouth of my five-year-old daughter. "Oh, no, none of that. The last time I went forward I barely came back. What if I get displaced in time and space and possibility? What if everything is different when I return?"

"We have to risk it. No more arguing. Go inside and do what has to be done."

"I'm going back to Juniper, but I'm not doing what you want. I'll figure out another approach."

Aelita said nothing, but merely regarded me with supernal calm certitude.

I strapped the kid into the car and locked the doors against any kind of kidnapping. Not likely in this ritzy neighborhood, but who could predict, amidst all this craziness?

An exhausted Juniper slumped semi-comatose on the couch, her long bare legs inviting. I fixed a couple of drinks for us, and she perked up. She actually brightened to the point of worrying about her hair and adjusting a shoulder strap.

"All right," I began. "Let's run down Holger's possible hideouts again—"

"Vern. That's your first name, isn't it? Vern, I'm very sad and I need you to kiss me."

The irony of my instant unfeigned reluctance was not lost on me. Just yesterday I had come here fantasizing about sex with my client, and now I was resisting any such offered pleasures.

"Really? Why now?"

"I didn't know you were a father before. Parenting is very sexy."

"Jesus . . . "

Her hands and mouth were all over me, and I couldn't stop her or myself.

I didn't think I'd have the energy for anything acrobatic after everything I had gone through, including making love just last night to Yulia. But the sex we had up and down that couch proved fabulous—right up to the end.

Blammo!

The DUCA future smelled bad. The omnipresent mat was rotting even more so than on my last visit. Did that mean I had jumped deeper into time? How could I be sure Holger Holtzclaw was even to be found in this era?

The ginormous animal skull was nowhere to be seen, so I just picked a random direction and started walking, naked as a mole rat.

After some indefinite period I saw what appeared to be a forest up ahead. But unlike on Perelandra, these organisms, I soon observed, were not separate entities, but merely extrusions of the mat, connected at their bases, of the same ill substance. Weird stalky mushroom-like excrescences, putrid and festering. I edged my way among them, feeling revulsion and disgust.

The tall tree trunks became more closely and randomly spaced, forming a kind of maze. After a while, I realized I could no longer discern the path I had taken.

Then I heard the weak call. "Help me. Someone help me, please."

Holger Holtzclaw—naked as myself, but battered and bruised— was immured in a living cage. I came up to his bars.

"Oh, thank God! I don't know who you are, or where I am, but you have to get me out of here!"

"I'm a detective. Your wife hired me to find you."

"Whatever she's paying you, I'll double it if you can free me!"

I studied the cage. I assumed Holger had tried to bend or bust the bars or dig through the mat without success. So I wasn't sure what I could do.

An image of the Green Lady suddenly filled my mind, vivid as if she were standing here before me. Could our mating have established some kind of bond between us?

I reached forth my hand, and as it approached the bars, the rancid stalks began to shiver and retreat from my presence.

Quickly employing my other hand, I created a gap big enough for the emaciated captive to slip through.

"Let's go! Quick!"

Trying to keep a straight course, we plunged through the forest, the slimy boles whapping us like the fabric flaps of a car wash.

Eventually, we emerged onto the undulant plain.

Motion attracted my eye upward.

Mister After All was arrowing toward us. He began to screech like a banshee.

At the same time, a big healthy-green sphere was rolling across the mat right at us.

"Run! Toward the beach ball!"

Mister After All almost got us. But just as his claw-like hands painfully yanked out strands of my hair, we plunged into the jade grass-smelling sphere like two raisins into a pudding, while Mister After All bounced off its surface that selectively repelled him.

The summery smell filled my lungs, and then my brain.

19 CANDY FROM A STRANGER

I HAD NEVER AWOKEN SIDE-BY-SIDE WITH A fellow sleeper before in the Vaalbara room at the AEOTA factory. I wondered if the management charged as much for a double as for a single.

I picked myself up in the familiar vacant cavernous room with the sunny rifts in the roof, then helped a stunned Holger Holtzclaw to his feet.

I was dressed in that morning's Oxford shirt and khakis. Holger wore what he had presumably worn on his visit to Thaumas & Company: a dapper summer-weight linen suit and Weejuns.

He looked around, blankly at first, then with growing awareness.

"I-I know this place. It's where I, where I—"

"Don't sweat it, man. We're safe now. Let's go."

We climbed the ladder and entered the anteroom.

There were two sets of my footprints in the dust: from my return after Green Lady sex and my return after Yulia sex. I added a third track as we made for the exit.

Unlike the previous loop, I was apparently not following right on the tail of myself. At least, my earlier avatar was nowhere to be seen.

He was probably already in the truck belonging to the Aeota Farms folks, winging his way back home.

The sun was fairly low in the east, and I had to hope that this was the morning of the pancake breakfast at the trailer. If it were earlier, the waiting would be frustrating. But if it were later—well, who could say what chances I would have missed?

I turned around to survey the ruins of the factory.

The signage atop the building said:

FIRST CHURCH OF THE GLORIFIED AEOTA
"EX NIHILO NIHIL FIT"

I turned back to Holger.

"You have a phone on you?"

He patted a coat pocket and came up with a smartphone.

"Can you get us an Uber?"

Holger was regaining some of his old Ponzi scheme *savoir-faire* as the harsh memories of his fantastical incarceration receded into a dream-like haze. "If I have a signal . . . "

The car took nearly an hour to arrive, out here in the middle of nowhere. During that time, I fed Holger a spontaneous bullshit story about drugs and kidnapping and industrial espionage. I was hardly about to tell him the truth—even assuming I really believed any of this madness. He seemed to buy my farrago.

"Juniper is going crazy without you," I concluded. "But you know that going back to her means facing the law."

Holger seemed genuinely repentant. Maybe his stint in the DUCA future, even rationalized as a nightmare, had actually served to rehabilitate him to some degree. I tried to imagine his lawyer making a case for "time served" at his sentencing hearing. "Although my client will not be incarcerated for another four billion years, he has actually already suffered through that imprisonment, and is thus exempt from additional punishment."

"I'll face the music," Holger said. "I'll make restitution and maybe the judge will be lenient. No one was really hurt."

"Good for you, pal. You've got a helluva woman in that Juniper."

My praise might have sounded a tad too intimately enthusiastic, because Holger eyed me askance.

"I mean, the money she laid out to find you and all. Plus the tears. Lots of tears."

Just then the Uber pulled up, and any suspicions were derailed. We climbed into the late-model car—which proved to be an Aeota Motors Protero.

The driver, a middle-aged white guy with a lean face and shaved head, wearing a T-shirt with Suzanne Vega's picture on it, introduced himself. "Hello. My name's Carnarvon Jarrell. Sit back and relax. We should be arrive at your destination in just a couple of hours, if the traffic is decent."

Holger and I both took the guy's advice. Suddenly I felt totally drained, and Holger seemed to experience the same enervation.

I drowsed dreamlessly until I heard Jarrell's polite coughing.

"We're almost there."

I looked around and saw we were on the final street leading to the Holtzclaw McMansion, but had yet to turn down the driveway.

"Stop here, please," I said.

We got out and Jarrell motored off.

"Is there a back entrance to the grounds?"

"Yes, for deliveries."

Give Holger credit for gratitude and trust; he didn't question me, his rescuer, but just followed meekly along.

I left Holger at the rear of the house.

"Don't leave this spot till I come and get you, understand? I have to prep Juniper for your startling reappearance."

And put my dick away, I didn't say.

I went around to the front of the house. Aelita sat patiently in the car.

Blammo!

I was back inside the house, merged with my earlier sweaty self, draped half-insensible atop a bent-over Juniper, her playsuit pooled around her ankles as she leaned against the back of the couch.

"You send me, girl, you really do. But now we gotta get dressed. I'm expecting a call that could break this whole investigation wide open."

Once dressed, I grabbed my old Nokia as if it were vibrating silently. "This could be it." I pretended to take the nonexistent call, conducting an imaginary dialogue.

"No! You say he should be arriving now? Fantastic!"

I hit the off button and addressed Juniper. "Go fix yourself up. Your hubby's coming up the drive."

She dashed off, and I went outside. I secured a meek and obedient Holger first, then got Aelita out of the car.

"Well done, Vern. I knew you could do it."

"If I have to wake up in that fucking place one more time, I'm going to stash my pajamas there ahead of any jumps."

The reunion between Holger and Juniper was suitably touching, even given knowledge of the cheating sex that had just occurred.

Aelita was tugging on my shirt again. "Get the thing he has for us. It's in his left coat pocket."

I asked Holger to hand over what he had in that location. Puzzled, he said, "But there's nothing—" Yet as he put his hand into his suit coat, he encountered something unexpected. He took it out and handed it to me.

It was a small transparent cellophane packet with a single largish lacquered crimson marble inside. The lettering said:

AEOTA CANDY COMPANY
FAMOUS HADES FIREBALL

I glared at Aelita.

Her beguiling child's face remained unperturbed. "Trust me," she said.

20 INVASION OF THE CHRONOSPORES

I NOTED THE CHANGES IN MY CITY AS WE DROVE away from the happily reunited Holtzclaw lovebirds. (I had made sure to tell them that they'd be getting my final bill in the mail, and that the total would be a significant five figures, even though I had no real faith in any of us surviving to pay or be paid. But old habits die hard. I figured that just before DUCA converted us all to slime, I'd probably still be instinctively checking the Nokia's voice mail for new clients.)

The downtown district, formerly several square blocks of empty storefronts and needle-strewn sidewalks populated by druggy wastrels was now host to flourishing emporiums and middle-class patrons. That was a plus. My continuum-skipping seemed to be following a gradient of improvement. We passed a beauty shop offering "Aeota Threading" and the Aeota Cinemas. The marquee on the latter advertised a double bill of THE GONE-AWAY WORLD and PORTRAIT OF JENNIE.

As I continued to drive toward Marty Quartz's apartment—or at least the place where I hoped he still lived—I saw other changes. There was a public park where there had never been one—the grassy acres were filled with people playing some kind of polo while driving electric-powered monowheels—and a tower that seemed to be sheathed in golden fish scales. Trouble was, I couldn't determine if these changes stemmed from my first, second, or third time-travel excursion. I wondered if I'd still have a home and a wife to return to after all this.

As if reading my thoughts, Aelita said in her alien way, "Don't worry, Yulia is okay."

"Thanks for that." A thought that had been bubbling under in my mind suddenly demanded voicing.

"I don't really understand about the nature of this change that DUCA is trying to install, this new monoculture regime. Shouldn't it be instantaneous, or have already happened? I mean, here we are, four billion years in DUCA's past. So he starts extending his realm backwards, conquering one antecedent year after another in succession as he moves toward uniting with LUCA, four billion years prior to our present. Shouldn't that wave of change have hit us by now? Or is it propagating at some finite speed, and has yet to engulf us? And is there some objective universal measure of time outside our normal reference frame that we can use to measure the advance of the threat? It's all highly confusing."

"None of your suppositions or conceptions are adequate or accurate. It's very hard to explain. A crude analogy involves tipping points and emergent phase shifts. Think of it like this. DUCA is sending spores backwards, to infest each previous era. And when those spores take root in a given period, they multiply until a critical mass is reached, at which point everything instantly transitions. It's like the 'false vacuum' theory in physics. The multiverse exists in an unstable mode that can be toppled over into an inescapable eternal lower-energy configuration by certain actions."

"These spores—what do they look like? How do they manifest?"

"You've already encountered one such manifestation, in the person of Brevis Baxter."

I had to pause to dredge up the associations with that name.

"You mean the crummy bum who braced me at A. O's Tea Room and gave me a box of goop?"

"Yes. He was a host to a DUCA spore, but not yet fully morphed. He was trying to contaminate you as well with that package. But I caused the spore to deliquesce before you could be affected."

"But I didn't even know you then! I didn't know any of this insanity existed."

"But I knew you already, Vern. And the 'insanity,' as you call it, or the reality, was always with you."

Stubbornly, I tried to remain optimistic. "I think the fact that we are still here talking, that DUCA hasn't yet colonized us, means that he will *never* colonize us, that he's already failed forever."

Aelita sighed. "I wish that were true, Vern. But it's not. We have to continue to struggle and fight, with all our brains and heart."

"Well, let's see what this lead that Marty uncovered is all about. Maybe it's a game-changer."

It was almost noon, my appointment time, when we pulled up in front of Marty Quartz's apartment building. Reassuringly, the place looked as I recalled, from however many timelines ago: a former tofu factory turned into luxury condos. Marty's job as a freelance IT security consultant paid good money, and allowed him to work just as much or little as he desired. We had met during another case, when I was tasked with finding the source of some industrial espionage.

In the lobby, a concierge rang Marty's room, then allowed us to proceed.

The door to Marty's third-floor quarters was already open when we arrived, and the man we had come to see awaited us, framed in that portal. Still dressed in yesterday's LARPing outfit of Irish tweeds and brogans, he resembled a plumper Yeats, right down to the little spectacles—which must have featured lenses of window glass, since Marty had never needed visual assistance till now, so far as I knew. His tired face and bleary eyes showed that his usquebaugh consumption had been authentically copious.

Seeing Marty, Aelita ran toward him and hurled herself at him as she had done for me when I arrived home.

"Uncle Marty!"

"Hey, microbe! What's fermenting?"

I did a double take. "Microbe?"

"You know, man. It's what Donald Duck calls his nephews."

"Oh, right . . . "

Inside the apartment, I sniffed a weird odor. It was organic, but not exactly that of the Archean period, I thought.

"What's that smell?"

"Oh, we had a peat fire going here last night for verisimilitude. Burning the bog, man. Getting in touch with the roots. Look, just let me change, and then we'll go."

"Go where?"

"A place I found when I Googled 'aeota.' One you never mentioned. Luckily, it's right here in town."

Marty disappeared in back, while Aelita and I waited silently. Upon his return, he sported his more customary outfit of cargo shorts, a baja "drug rug" hoodie in eye-straining rainbow colors, and Teva sandals.

Down in the car, Marty sat in the back rather than fuss with Aelita's booster seat. Obviously feeling more alive after some covert bedroom toot, possibly of a trendy restorative nutraceutical, he leaned forward in his typical energetic fashion to tell what he knew.

"This guy's been on my radar for a while. Roopnarine Ströma. Heads Ströma Heuristic Systems. Took over the business from his father, Aadidev, the founder. Sells software-learning systems to the government and big corporations. DARPA's a client. But I never realized he's got a side project that's been going on for decades. It's called AEOTA. Stands for 'Artilect Enjoined to Operate on Thomist Axioms.'"

"In English, please."

"An artificial intelligence designed to reason about God and the universe."

"Okay. Not too ambitious."

"I figure, given the coincidence of names, that this gizmo might have some answers to any questions you can ask it."

"And Ströma will see us?"

"Yeah, he knew my work and agreed. I didn't explain that you were nuts, though."

"Thanks. When I'm running the universe, I'll do something nice for you in return."

"Hey, that reminds me. Let me see that phone of yours a minute."

I passed the Nokia over my shoulder.

"Can't see any sign of modding. And you say it printed out a slip of paper?"

"Twice. I've got them right in my pocket."

Marty handed back my phone. "We'll look into this later."

The building housing Ströma Heuristic Systems was a sleek early-eighties postmodern edifice on the edge of town. It reminded me generically of the AEOTA HQ upstate, and I had to repress a shiver.

Roopnarine Ströma was a striking, handsome young figure. Of

blended ethnicities—I was going to guess, based on his name, half-Hindu, half-Swedish—he presented a dapper businessman's façade with an overlay of intellectual heft. Very Richard Branson by way of Elon Musk.

After shaking hands all around, even with a somber and wide-eyed Aelita, Ströma conducted us deep into the bowels of the place, past layers of security.

"When my father first began to construct and program AEOTA, he didn't want to use any of the company's then-limited resources on his private mission. Stockholders and venture capitalists get antsy about that. So the project was tucked away in a basement room, functioning on whatever he could scrounge, and it's stayed there ever since. We don't dare move it, because we would have to power it down, and no one knows if it would ever reboot. It's the most massive kludge I've ever seen."

As he told us this, Ströma unlocked a final door and swung it wide, and I could instantly see he wasn't kidding.

21 INTERVIEW WITH AEOTA, INTERVIEW WITH AN ARTIST

THE ROOM WAS NOT LARGE, PROBABLY ABOUT AS big as the kitchen in the Holtzclaw McMansion. It was air-conditioned and featured a false floor for easy access to cables. In the middle was an old beat-up workbench. The long metal table supported a mass of what looked to be randomly gathered computer hardware piled high, threaded together with a variety of wires, the whole mess surrounded by tipsy functioning stacks of other equipment, some in racks, some in freestanding towers, leaving just about enough room for three adults and a kid to crowd inside. Ströma closed the door and locked it.

The many LED telltale lights—red, green, amber, and blue— reminded me of a nighttime jungle scene with the eyes of animals shining in the gloom. At the center bottom of the silicon ziggurat on the table was a monochrome display and a clunky keyboard. The ancient equipment triggered a memory I had not considered in ages: my first computer as a kid, a Commodore 64.

"Is that . . . "

Ströma seemed embarrassed. "Yes, it's a Cee Sixty-four. You have to remember that Dad started building this monstrosity circa 1985. By the time he died, he had added about six million layers of equipment around the Commodore. But the Sixty-four is still the kernel and the interface."

I walked closer to the blank screen. Its mute blinking cursor seemed both mocking and beckoning.

"What do I do?"

"Just type something."

My fingers on the keyboard reactivated the body memories of playing crude videogames, using arrow keys to manipulate pixel creatures that only a child's imagination could invest with a semblance of life.

—*Hello. Are you Aeota?*

—*Yes, I am one Aeota.*

—*Can you tell me how to defeat the Dark Archon?*

—*Since act is perfection, it is not limited except through a potency which itself is a capacity for perfection.*

Ströma had been reading over my shoulder. "That's pure Aquinas, Dad's favorite philosopher. He programmed AEOTA with the entire canon, from the *Summa Theologica* on down. But it's not like a chatbot. It doesn't just regurgitate text. It's told me some things . . . "

Ströma paused, as if to say more would be too unsettling or incriminating.

The history lesson Ströma had just delivered suggested a different line of questioning to me, for which I was grateful, since I was just fumbling around like a blind guy with a Rubik's Cube.

—*Is Aeota a god? Is DUCA a god?*

—*Neither is the Prime Mover nor First Cause.*

—*Then DUCA can be defeated?*

—*Neither matter nor form have being of themselves, nor are they produced or corrupted of themselves.*

This high-flown dialogue was getting old fast.

—Tell me how I can save the world.

—The will does not precede the intellect but follows upon it.

—That doesn't help!

—I need more input.

—More input? Like what?

AEOTA did not respond.

"Goddamn it!" Frustrated, I kicked the table leg.

My action dislodged something from its niche among the equipment. The small object fell until the tether of its cable, left dangling in midair, stopped it.

I plucked it up. The thing was a bulky vintage light pen, usually used for drawing directly onto a CRT screen in the days before tablets.

Aelita said, "Daddy, I think the machine is telling you that it wants you to show it something new."

Marty looked dubious. "That relic's not a scanner, man."

A queer impulse made me dig in my pants pocket. I came up with the two slips of paper that my Nokia had outputted. I smoothed them out on a small bare patch of tabletop, then drew the light pen slowly across each one in turn.

The eight emojis appeared on the monochrome screen in full color, all in a line. They spun like the icons on an old-school slot machine, then disappeared.

AEOTA displayed a street address on its screen, then a final message.

—Toward the time of the judgment the sun and moon will be darkened in very truth. My work here is done.

The screen went black.

Ströma looked at me with an initial incredulity that swiftly built to anger.

"You broke it. You killed AEOTA."

I felt guilty, but wasn't about to admit any culpability. "Hey, anybody who ever watched a single episode of *Star Trek* could have predicted this outcome."

I thought it would be expedient to leave before Ströma decided to have my head on a platter, so I grabbed up the slips of paper from the table.

Now they were blank.

I kept them nonetheless.

I thought that maybe Marty Quartz would have insisted on coming with Aelita and me to the address that AEOTA had given us, but he surprised me by asking to be delivered home.

"I had a long night, Vern. I'm beat. And frankly, this weird quest of yours is creeping me out. I figure you'll let me know how things shake out, one way or another."

"Oh, you'll know soon enough whether I succeed or not—along with the rest of the world."

Alone with Aelita in the car, heading across town, I said, "Who do you think is at this address?"

"Someone to help us, not someone to harm us."

"That's reassuring. What makes you say that?"

"Nothing but a feeling."

"No superior superhuman knowledge?"

"I'm just a little girl."

"And I'm the last of the Romanovs."

The address proved to belong to a simple moss-green ranch house in an innocuous suburb north of the city. Tidy lawn, old-fashioned curtains. I rang the bell with Aelita holding my hand.

The door opened, and after a puzzled second, I realized I had cause to lower my glance.

An old woman in a wheelchair had revealed herself. Dressed neatly yet not too fussily, she exhibited a keen gaze and general alertness that was the opposite of any kind of maundering senility. A gentle smile graced her face. I was reminded of a Mother Superior or some other emblematic matriarch. Her aged features appeared familiar to me in some fashion, but I could not immediately place them.

"Yes, how can I help you?"

"I'm not sure."

The woman regarded Aelita and smiled. "My name's Priscilla. What's yours?"

"Aelita."

"That's very like the name of another little girl I know. One named Aeota."

Dumbfounded, I asked, "What's your last name?"

"Cohen."

"You're Pris Cohen. You do my daughter's favorite comic book."

"Write and draw, yes. I assumed that was why you were here. I often receive visits from fans."

"Yes, of course. Could we come in?"

"Certainly."

Priscilla rolled backwards, and we entered. She spun her wheelchair deftly about and scooted off. We followed.

The living room served as her studio. A drafting table with an unfinished page pinned to it filled most of the space, along the raw materials of her trade and a host of inspirational sculptures and toys and dolls and other tchotchkes.

"I'm afraid I can't offer you any refreshments. Tomorrow is my shopping day, and the larder's bare. But I suspect that you're not here for cookies and milk."

"No, we're not. We need desperately to know all about Aeota. What can you tell us?"

"I was the original Aeota, you know. The inspiration. My uncle, Herbert Crowley, drew the Wigglemuch strip."

I did some quick calculations. "That's not possible. You'd have to be—"

"I am one-hundred-and-fifteen years old."

"You don't look a day over one-oh-five."

Priscilla ignored my feeble witticism. "After I reached adolescence and my uncle died, I never thought much about my early role as an Alice Liddell–type figure. But my uncle's drawing career must have inspired me. I spent my whole adult professional employment as a graphic artist in the advertising field. Afterwards, I lived a quiet retired life as a weekend painter. But then, recently, memories of Aeota began to recur to me, and I felt inspired to continue my uncle's comic strip in monthly format. I was lucky enough to find a publisher, and here we are."

"But aren't you channeling messages from the real Aeota?"

"Who might she be?"

"She's LUCA, or the Green Lady—I think. We're fighting DUCA. He wants to conquer all of time and space."

Priscilla smiled at me with a mix of benevolence and pity. "I'm sure this all means something to you, young man. But I fear it's got nothing to do with me nowadays—if it ever did"

I turned to Aelita. "You can convince her, Lita. Just tell her we need her help."

Desperation was driving me. I felt suddenly at the end of my rope. How many more blind alleys did I have to stumble down before this nightmare was over?

"I can't do anything, Daddy. She knows better than me. I'm sorry."

I looked back to the old lady. She had ceased smiling, and the lines of her face were relaxed into a webwork of wrinkles.

And her incompetent lips revealed a slice of her teeth.

22 Go with the Flow

"You're my daughter."

As soon as the words emerged, I realized how insane I sounded. But the reaction of both my daughter and Priscilla Cohen confirmed my crazy revelation.

"Yes, Daddy, she's me. One of me. And she knows so much more. That's why I'm not pressing her for help. Whatever's ahead, she's already been through it, and so she knows just what to do now."

The old dame regarded me with a placid humble majesty. I was reminded of the Green Lady's quiet but vibrant charisma. I just hoped nobody expected me to have sex with this old bat as well. Not that I was necessarily morally against it, just that I was tired of being led around by my dick.

Pris Cohen's voice exhibited no regrets or hesitancy. "I cannot affirm what you say. But I cannot deny it either. The truth is both and neither. So you will just have to trust me."

Trust me. The same request Aelita had made when I looked dubiously at the Famous Hades Fireball candy that Holger Holtzclaw had brought back from the far future. (I patted my pocket and found the round packet still there.) Could I trust either of them? Hadn't everyone involved in this hallucinatory affair taken me for a ride? But what choice did I have?

"Okay, you've got my trust. But only on the installment plan. So, what next?"

Priscilla looked at her slim silver wristwatch. "Just wait. It will only be minutes now."

Aelita walked over to the old lady in the wheelchair and climbed onto her lap. Priscilla hugged her in grandmotherly fashion, and Aelita returned the embrace. Their faces, side by side, old and young, further cemented the truth of their unique kinship.

I walked over to the drawing board and studied the unfinished artwork. A "splash page," one big panel, the deft pencil work depicted the heroine Aeota, expectant on some shore and faced with a tsunami, a huge wave clotted with debris that threated to cascade down upon her, surely crushing all life from her. But the comic-book girl's unfinished face suggested resolve and certitude of ultimate victory.

Someone started banging on the front door, hammering at it with what sounded like a succession of small watermelons fired from an air cannon. I moved toward the entrance, but before I could take more than a couple of steps the door crashed inward, hanging from one hinge.

A small squad of semi-human creatures flowed chaotically in.

The front one wore the gnarly face of Brevis Baxter—but a face composed now of shoddy putrescence.

Back at Arturo Olvidado's bar, when he had passed over the contaminant spore package to me, Baxter had resembled a crusty hobo, a burnt-out case, unwashed, wasted and trashed, but undeniably human. Now he looked like what a simpleton child, asked to represent the human figure, might assemble out of moldy cottage cheese and twigs. His companions, though sporting different countenances, mimicked this variegated but essentially monotone look.

I realized that Baxter was now composed entirely of DUCA substance, coarse maritime glop threaded with fibers and particles. His entire cellular makeup, as well as his clothing, had been transformed into the far-future slime. Here, then, was the beginning onslaught that Aelita had warned me about, the massing of the constituent grains of sand that would eventually avalanche our universe into DUCA's desired state.

Baxter's companions moved toward Aelita and Priscilla, while Baxter himself blocked me from coming to their aid. The convert to DUCA spoke in a voice even more grotty than his previous one, his kelp vocal chords straining to reproduce human language.

"Mister Thaumas wants you and the girl."

"My interest in seeing your boss is zilch."

"You will come."

Baxter laid a hand on me, and it was like the heavy wet weight of a waterlogged corpse descending to implacably clamp my flesh. No wonder he and his pals had been able to batter the door down.

Another of the DUCA-men plucked Aelita out of Priscilla Cohen's lap. Neither my daughter nor her other self resisted.

Another hench-thing croaked, "The old lady?"

"We do not need her," replied Baxter.

Three of the creatures flopped themselves atop Priscilla like so many soggy mattresses, losing their individual definition in a pig pile. They writhed and squelched and squeezed for about ninety seconds, before retreating and reverting to their separate components.

Priscilla Cohen was gone, her wheelchair dripping with slime.

I expected Aelita to cry out or show some emotion, but she

remained stolid and seemingly unconcerned. But I felt Priscilla Cohen's absence like a rip in the fabric of reality.

Outside, a windowless van labeled AEOTA DELIVERY SERVICE blocked my car. Into it all but three of the monsters surged: Baxter, still gripping my arm, and two creatures to guard Aelita. I supposed I should have been incensed that they regarded my kid as the more dangerous of us two.

Baxter hustled me into the driver's seat of my own car, afterwards quickly slipping into the shotgun position, his malleable vegetable butt simply configuring itself to engulf the projecting booster seat. The two cronies cradling Aelita between them oozed into the rear.

"Drive," said Baxter.

"Where?"

"You know the place."

"AEOTA HQ?"

"Yes."

I tried to recall what the empty factory had promoted itself to be the last time I had passed through, but couldn't remember.

"But that site's empty."

"Not now it isn't."

"Can I just call my wife first, and tell her we'll be late? She'll be worried."

"No. There is no need. You won't be late. You will be never."

23 RETURN TO AEOTA

THE BY-NOW FAMILIAR ROUTE TO AEOTA HQ—
how many times had I gone back and forth along this stretch in
just the past two days?—had been transmogrified beyond all
comprehension.

The changes became apparent as soon as we pulled away from
Priscilla's house, which had remained an oasis of stability. (But even
as we proceeded a few yards down her street, I could see in my rearview mirror that the forces of change had begun their assault on her
house as well.) The abnormalities were, at first, intermittent, inter-
spersed with irregularly situated and irregularly bordered expanses
of normality. But the closer we got to our destination, the more the
abhorrent transformations tended to predominate.

Many of the citizens we passed in the city had also morphed to
full DUCA-hood. But unlike this crew of hired roughnecks that had
come to capture me and Aelita, the alteration to their personages
had not inspired any obvious devilry. Seemingly unaware of their
debased natures, they slorped and blarfed along the DUCAfied
pavement like so many human-shaped blancmanges, conducting
their mundane errands, ambulatory piles of ocean wrack: Sargasso
mailmen, housewives, businessmen, students and shopkeepers. A

jogger trotted by, littering her path with dislodged wet bits of her pelagic body. A teenager texted away on a phone that was composed of the same material as its body, and which seemed fused to its hand. Behind the wheel of a car, the gray-green driver idly tapped a boneless floppy striated hand in time to the music of its radio.

But beyond the people, the landscape, both natural and man-made, had altered as well.

As in the forest where Holger Holtzclaw had been imprisoned, all the vegetation in the bad patches emerged seamlessly from the tainted substrate, mere extrusions of DUCA. The birds and squirrels in their branches were DUCA-forms too.

And many of the buildings, large and small, as well as lampposts, billboards, and traffic lights, had fallen victim to the spreading stain. The smaller structures seemed semi-stable, wavering slightly under the unnatural stresses of maintaining their forms with such unsuitable material. But the bigger, multistory buildings swayed and oscillated like Jell-O sculptures in an earthquake, appearing ready to snap and rupture and fall at any minute. Nonetheless, people continued to stream in and out of the banks and hotels and offices.

A defeatist thought jumped up in my head. Was humanity really any worse off than before? I recalled my impressions during my first forest-fire-tinged trip when it felt as if civilization were collapsing. Maybe this kind of slimy rapture was the best we could hope for, given the human condition and our ability to screw things up.

Then I remembered Aelita's simple innocent joy in seeing me come home, and knew that the answer was no, mankind wasn't better off as DUCA's slaves.

Not that there was much I could do about it at the moment.

I thought once or twice about pulling over to the curb as we passed through the normal areas and leaping from the car and running for help. But Brevis Baxter had one sloppy arm around my shoulder, and I was certain that with his strength and speed he could strangle me instantly at my first false move.

And then of course there was Aelita to worry about, cushioned between the two monsters in the back. I kept angling my mirror to check on her. She never once showed a trace of alarm or fear or concern. That was my girl.

When we passed the city limits and were out in the countryside, the changes persisted. It was no less alarming to see long seaweed-textured pastures full of DUCA cows.

And the prevalence of the contamination became almost universal.

A familiar barn caught my eye. It was the Aeota Farm where Philip Kendrick Langham and Martha Washington ran their egg business. Totally swamped with DUCA's influence, the place reminded me of a Lovecraft tale I had not considered since those college days, a story whose name I could no longer recall.

Langham and Washington themselves stepped out of their farmhouse as we passed, all sloppy smiling briny heaps, and waved.

I finally broke my appalled silence.

"Aelita, honey—are you all right?"

"I'm fine, Daddy. Don't worry. Everything is going to be okay."

Brevis Baxter unfurled a glutinous laughter like a hippo farting through wet cement, and his buddies joined in.

Making the last turn to the site of AEOTA HQ, I wasn't sure what to expect. The flourishing postmodern enterprise I had first visited, or the empty shell where I kept waking up after my time trips.

But neither aspect obtained.

Occupying an enormous footprint of land was the incredible mega-skull from the far future of Mister After All. But instead of rearing starkly bone-white, it too showed itself to be formed entirely of the DUCA rot.

Atop the skull, the AEOTA signage proclaimed the skull's current tenants.

We emerged from the parked car and walked toward the door.

"At least let me hold my daughter's hand."

"Oh ho! How dumb do you think we are? No, there'll be none of that monkey business."

We passed through a sloppy bulging parody of a door and entered a facsimile of the atrium. The same receptionist seen during my first visit was there, but of course only as a gruesome avatar of her former gorgeous self. Her equally dire coworkers came and went.

Without necessity for clearance, Baxter and his buddies brought me and Aelita into the wobbly upper-floor office of Thomas Totenwelt Thaumas.

Seated behind his desk on his fancy scooter, the man no longer resembled Judge Hardy so much as he looked like Mister After All. How I could not have seen the resemblance earlier, I couldn't say.

"Mister Ruggles! You return to us. How nice. And with your very welcome little girl. I know someone who is most eager to meet her. He has been waiting forever to get his hands on her."

Trying to unnerve Thaumas, I said, "I see you've come a long way in totalizing your affinities."

Thaumas's face registered genuine puzzlement, insofar as those coarse features could.

"What nonsense are you on about?"

"The name of your organization." I dredged up the acronym, which I had heard after all just about thirty-six hours ago. "The Association of Engineering Ontologists Totalizing Affinities."

"But that is not what our brand stands for at all! We are producers of Architecturally Engineered Organisms for Terraforming Alternities. All the splendid new constituents of the material world which you see about you come straight from our labs."

"Are you deranged? You didn't create any of this. It's all DUCA's doing, as he floods the past with his essence."

Thaumas triggered his intercom. "Ms. Bagasse, would you please have Dr. Ponto come in?"

Within half a minute, the formerly beautiful secretary—who now smelled less like a florist shop and more like a pile of imperfectly devoured crab shells under a hot sun—ushered in Microbial Matt, the bastard who had pushed me off the ledge and started this whole mad odyssey.

"Hey, Vern, good to see you. You're back for another tour, I take it."

I lunged at Ponto, but was almost immediately brought up short by Brevis Baxter.

"Dr. Ponto, please tell our guests about the various organisms we have bred to perfect the environment."

Ponto launched into some gobbledygook that I paid no attention to. My mind was frantically scrabbling about the confines of its cage for a way out of this. If only I could grab ahold of Aelita, maybe she could send us away from here somehow, as when her Archean counterpart had blasted me off to Venus.

Now Thaumas was talking again. "So you must assuredly now admit, Mister Ruggles, that there is no need to invoke imaginary entities who are responsible for these wondrous changes. All such conceptions are delusions on your part. Your mind is defective, or you would surely concede the truth. Occam's razor still applies. The simplest answer is most likely correct. There are no fanciful creatures at the far origin and ending of our world, directing our destiny, contending for dominance. LUCA and DUCA, what is there to choose between them? No, there is only science, here and now."

"If there's only your perverted human science, then who are you working for? Who wants my daughter?"

"I didn't say anyone wants your daughter, did I?"

"Yes, you dirty fucker, you did!"

Thaumas motored out in his chair from behind his desk. His identity with Mister After All had solidified even more unmistakably.

"Let me have a closer look at her. Maybe she *could* be of some use to us. What a sweet little child she is. And very talented too, no doubt, with such a smart father."

Aelita remained unmoved by Thaumas's approach. But she inexplicably began to whine.

"Daddy, I'm hungry! Don't you have anything for me?"

"C'mon, Aelita, drop the kiddy act! Do something! Please, before it's too late."

"I'm hungry, Daddy! Anything, please! Even just a candy—"

The Famous Hades Fireball seemed to leap from my pocket into my hand. I popped the sealed inflated cellophane and the crimson sphere shot out across the space between Aelita and me like a missile.

With her hands pinned by her guards, she snapped it out of the air like a dog with a snack or a trained seal with a fish.

And then we were outta there faster than light.

24 HORN, OM, SUN, HOME

LYING FLAT, I OPENED MY EYES AFTER AN indefinite period of unconsciousness, sensed and saw that I was naked under an empty sky. Turning my head, I regarded Aelita and found her in the same condition. And as on my first visit to the Archean, I could see that she was not precisely my daughter, not a little girl but rather some other more ancient vessel who shared a spiritual and physical kinship with my child.

A warmish sun shone down on us, and I was so excited and relieved to be out of the grip of Thaumas and his crew that I jumped up happily to my feet, and took in the wider view.

I couldn't believe it. We were not in the healthy primordial Archean. We had been transported to DUCA's dying era, four billion years in the future. The pustulant pestilence that had invaded my age was everywhere, just as on my last visit. Not aggressively occupying many different forms, true, yet still quietly dominant and universal.

Aelita had come to her feet. She looked utterly subdued.

"What happened?" I demanded. "Why are we here? I thought that Fireball was our ticket to your home, where we could regroup or something."

For the first time, Aelita sounded weary. "It was supposed to be. But the fact that we are here means that the Dark Archon has become too strong. We were too late. He's won. There is nothing left except for us to acknowledge our defeat."

Her words pained me horribly. I grabbed her by her slim child's shoulders and shook her. "No! We can't give up. There must be something more we can do!"

"There is not."

I slumped. "So you'll just surrender to him when he shows up?"

"That is my only plan."

"Well, I'm not going down without a fight!"

I looked about the monoscape frantically for some sort of weapon, but of course there was nothing. Were these seaweed strands strong enough to use as a garrote? I bent down and tried to disentangle and rip out a length of the crappy fabric.

"DUCA arrives."

Mister After All was levitating down from the heavens. When I could distinguish his wizened face, I saw it was beaming with vicious satisfaction.

He alighted upon the infinite raft about five or six yards away from us. He beckoned to my daughter.

"You must come to me now."

I yelled something wordless and hurled myself upon him.

The Dark Archon batted me aside as if I were a shuttlecock. The force of the blow left me dazed. I thought maybe I had some busted ribs. I tried to lever myself up, but only made it halfway.

Aelita was walking calmly to meet Mister After All. And with every step she aged.

From five years old she passed through adolescence and young womanhood in just a few paces, becoming mature and beautiful.

In only seconds, I got to experience what my daughter would have grown up into, all the stages of her maturation. She reminded me of the Green Lady in her flush of vitality. As she continued to walk, she continued to age. Her twenties passed in a step or two, then she was into her middle age.

By the time she stood face to face with Mister After All, she looked exactly like the venerable Priscilla Cohen.

The old woman looked down at me. "Goodbye, Daddy. Trust me still."

A triumphant DUCA said nothing. He merely enfolded Aelita in his embrace. But his embrace did not stop when his arms met. His form flowed and expanded until he was a faceless blanket enveloping Aelita, just as his protean minions had engulfed the other Priscilla.

A similar obscene humping peristalsis worked upon the swaddled Aelita until she was fully dissolved and absorbed. She never made a sound, my little girl, as she vanished into the gullet of a sterile futurity. Then Mister After All pulled himself back into his human semblance.

He leered down at me. "Now she is mine forever. You, I leave here to perish."

Mister After All made as if to surge into the sky.

But he found himself rooted.

His feet were anchored in a pool of brilliant healthy vibrant green substance.

He jerked up first one leg without being able to disengage from the elastic stuff, then the other.

"No! This cannot be!"

The green wave flowed up his body, and at the same time radiated outward across the microbial mat. Faster and faster it spread, until all was an Archean, Perelandrian green from horizon to horizon.

Seemingly by sheer force of will DUCA had halted the green while just a few square inches of his bald crown remained unconverted. His eyes bulged and his mouth gaped helplessly.

But the green blew past his last defenses, and he was entirely swamped.

He began to melt away, subsumed into the microbial mat, until he was just a pair of desperate eyes embedded in the raft. Then those too were gone.

My ribs still ached. Nonetheless I crawled to where Mister After All had vanished. Sobbing, stroking the surface with my palm to invoke some sign of Aelita, I called her name over and over.

But there was no response. My daughter was gone forever.

When I gave up, a curious wave of heaviness began to creep along my limbs, until it finally filled my brain with sleep.

And I awoke and found me here on the cold hillside.

Well, it wasn't actually cold, and the patch of sun-kissed grass was flat. But that famous line captured what I felt.

I was lying, all clothed, in a woodland clearing next to my car. Beautiful, multiplex reality was restored, thanks to Aelita's sacrifice.

The whole world seemed normal.

Or at least as normal as it ever tended to be.

Standing up, I felt great.

No structure associated with AEOTA, neither mega-skull nor factory, reared in this spot. Instead, from the natural clearing a dirt road arrowed off, presumably leading back to the paved highway.

A quick recon showed no traces of anyone here with me, now or in the obvious past. I had no option but to get in my car and drive off, alone, without the child who had accompanied me.

Average traffic greeted me on the highway. I pointed my car toward the city.

Partway home, I saw a familiar farm. But the spiffy unadorned barn did not bear the ghost sign proclaiming CHEW AEOTA PLUG. I pulled into the property.

Philip Kendrick Langham and Martha Washington emerged, smiling.

"Hey, dude, what's up?"

"Is this Aeota Farm? Do you sell eggs?"

"Afraid we can't help you with that, bro. That's not us. El and Double-You Floral. We raise tulips. Wholesale only."

"All right then. Thanks anyhow. Good luck with everything."

I didn't dare return to the trailer where Yulia lived, nor to my own apartment. So I went to my office. The familiar key worked and I let myself gratefully inside.

I surely deserved a drink. But there was no booze anywhere in the office, not even an empty bottle in the trash. After searching every niche, I suddenly realized that the old compulsion to swig some tequila at every opportunity had left me, as if a tub full of dirty water had finally ebbed down the drain.

My Nokia weighed heavily in my pocket. I used it to call Marty Quartz.

"Marty, it's me, Vern. You won't believe what happened after Aelita and I left you."

"Whoa man, slow down. After you and who left who?"

"After I broke Ströma's artificial intelligence. He's not going to sue us, is he?"

"I have no idea what you've been smoking, my lad, but you could have been kind enough to share it."

"But I . . . Never mind. I'll talk to you later."

I powered up my desktop computer and checked today's date.

It was sixteen months before I had ever Googled "aeota."

I did so now again.

Zero hits.

My Nokia rang, almost sending me through the ceiling.

The voice of my lawyer, Herb Scroup, said, "Vern, hello, how ya doing? Listen, I need you in the office to sign these papers for the divorce. Yulia's guy is on my ass about it. We can't put it off any longer."

"Burn them."

"What?"

"Burn the papers. I'm going home."

The doublewide did not display the neatness of my last visit, nor the shabbiness of my abandonment years. Nor was there a tricycle or any kid's toys lying about. Rather, the whole scene seemed to teeter on a knife's edge of possibilities, with a different outcome awaiting on either side.

I banged on the door like a madman. Yulia came quickly. Her face did not exactly register glee at my manifestation on her doorstep.

"Oh, it's you, Vern. What do you want?"

"Yulia, baby, it's not what I want. It's not what you want. It's what the universe wants. We have to get back together."

Suspicion warred with hope in her face. "I thought you gave up the booze."

"I did, I did. Or I will. Whatever. Our wishes don't really matter. What matters is us starting a family. We really need to have a kid. Everything depends on it!"

Yulia tried to compose her face into a stern mask. But her incompetent lips only made her look adorable—as adorable as our unborn daughter. "You'd better come in out of the sun, Vern. But just for a minute. No funny stuff. We're still separated, remember, even if the divorce hasn't happened yet."

"It's not gonna happen, believe me." I felt the Nokia vibrate with an incoming text.

"Just let me get this, Yule. Then we'll sit down and really talk."

The unexpected text read:

herald unity today at home

Followed by:

PRINT TEXT Y/N?

I chose YES, and the phone spat out its impossible fortune-cookie slip.

I handed the paper to Yulia. She studied it, then looked quizzically at me.

"What's it mean?"

"Baby, that's just what we're gonna find out!"